THE SHIELD

RA'UN SETI

ISBN 978-1499796759

Introduction

He awoke quickly staring out in between the window shutter from the head of his bed. The darkened room crammed with dusty beer bottles and playboy magazines. He suddenly noticed a male figure standing at the front of his window, not thinking he jumps to his feet and immediately rushes to the window. "Hey whoever you are you need to get away from here!" he shouted. "Damn crack head," he muttered to himself stumbling back to his bed. Seconds later a spray of bullets filled the area as dust particles dance in a blade of light that squeezed through a missing window shutter. "Shit!" he cries nervously ducking to the floor as he scribbles desperately for his piece beneath the bed mattress. "You're not going to find it boy" the sound of a male voice creeps up behind him. Suddenly he tries to turn around to see who was speaking. "Don't move!" as he hears the clicking noise of a gun hammer being pulled back. "On your feet slowly," the gunman replied.

All he could do was stand upright perfectly still staring

at the dresser in front of him. "Who are you, and what

do you want from me?"

"Nothing," the gunman replied coldly. "Then why is you

doing this I haven't done anything to you have I?"

"No not directly put to others you have, so I'm here to

revenge their pain and suffering that you have caused."

"What are you saying?" asked the frighten man as he

tries slowly to turn and face his intruder. "Don't move

I'm warning you punk, don't let me say it again," said

the gunman now pressing the point of the gun in the

back of the young man head. "Please don't kill me."

"Ah it's funny to hear people like you beg, it makes me

feel good knowing that I'm making a difference."

"Who do you think you are the batman of the ghetto? You think that you can save the world or something?"

"No, not the world my friend, just the ghetto," the gunman replied. "You are fucking crazy nigga!" the gunman laughed. "That is what all my victims said just before I stuck my knife into their skull. But unfortunately for you tonight you won't die from the point of my blade but at the point of this thirty-eight slug…."

<u>Chapter 1</u>

Leroy walked into the precinct just as the Monday shift got underway. He went quickly to his desk and didn't say good morning to anyone. He wasn't even supposed to be on the property. "What's up Leroy is you here to get on your knees and beg for your job back?" someone asked. A couple of people standing around laughed. Leroy ignored them and started going through his desk drawer. He tossed aside an old box of condoms, a Tupac CD, pencils, some old set of playing cards, and newspaper clippings. "Shit!" he began digging furiously and then stopped. "That's it." he picked up a small picture of him, with his daughter, and baby momma. He was about to bounce when he saw a stack of loaded messages on his answering machine. "Leroy I need you to – click'. Leroy scanned through the messages quickly to see who had tried to reach him during the four days he was gone. He knew there was really nothing much he could do now after being fired from his job. He wouldn't return any of the calls unless it was something helpful in solving a case.

It was a nice cool Monday and he had planned to take his daughter Kametica to the Mecklenburg County Park to feed the ducks. While working a homicide case of an ex-gang member from Dodge City by the name of Ray Hill, he had browsed through a convenient store and bought a box of crackers and held it just for such an occasion. The past few weeks had turned into an unexpected layoff. As far Leroy was concerned he wouldn't have to deal with, drive by shootings, gang members killing each other over turf. No word of who's pushing what around the city. Leroy felt a hand touch his right arm. "What's up Leroy?" said Belinda. "You don't believe in staying home do you? I came by your house ten times I even left about a dozen messages on your answering machine." Belinda spends a lot of her time in the office doing paper work these days with homicide cases reaching a record high in the district of Charlotte she finds herself working the streets more in the last six months than in the previous two years combined. She felt a little out of touch with the streets. "I wanted to tell K.T. to stake out in front of your house but I couldn't afford to pay his lazy ass," she said. "I don't work at this dump anymore don't you remember?" her hand still on his right arm Belinda politely moves it away. "Just came in here to see how you were doing." Leroy stroked his salt-and-pepper afro a left over from his days in training. He kept it short and trimmed in contrast to his goatee of unruly black hair. "Now whose fault is that?" Belinda asked. She looked around to see if anyone was listening. "You can't go around cussing the boss out and calling him an Uncle Tom to his face, are you crazy?"

"Well he is an Uncle Tom, an ugly one at that! So what do you want from me Belinda?"

"He wants to squash the beef, he wants you to come back."

"When today?"

"Yes, I'm not supposed to tell you this but he is willing to give you a job as head detective."

"You can tell him he is still an Uncle Tom. I bust my black ass for this department and he can't handle me calling him a name so he goes and fires me. That's bullshit and you know it Belinda," he waved his arms wildly. "You know what I need the time off."

"You already had enough time off," Belinda said. Leroy smiled and shook his head and started towards the door when Belinda cut in front of him. "Okay now I have done my part for the Captain, now here is what's going on," she motioned for Leroy to follow her into the interrogation room. The walls were gray with hard wooden floors, a long black table stood in the center with white plastic chairs around it. A video camera hung from the corner of the ceiling. "I believe we have a serial killer on our hands. We didn't discover this until a couple of days ago. That's when we tried to contact you." Leroy rubbed his hand over his head and down his face. "Linkage?"

"Black males, shot, stabbed, and beaten. The photos are horrifying, the stuff that he did to these young men." Belinda laid a file on the table in front of Leroy. "The amount of damage he done to these guys is overwhelming, here see for yourself." Leroy went through the photos and stopped at one in particular. "Wow, twenty five, black male, he looks mess up." Leroy studied the photos, closed his eyes and then shook his head. "I have another file in my office, a Robert Lee Maxwell, want to check it out?" Leroy nodded. "We have tons of photos." Belinda continued. "And our guy left something behind that is going to trip you out, you can see it in some of the photos. Maybe you didn't catch it, but you can see the funny blue drawing on the victim's arms and legs."

"What do you think it mean?" asked Leroy.

"Well, at first I thought that it was something to do with some gang mess. But he was telling us something and we weren't listening."

 "What's that?"

 "I'm not sure, the first victim Rodney Bell was found in the bathroom. The area was clean, no water or crap around except a red bible on the floor with little bible verses all over the walls written in the victims own blood." Leroy sat silently listening. "Second murder a body was found in the basement with a white substance beneath his fingertips. Investigators confirmed that it was crack-cocaine, a bible was found on the floor with shredded bible pages on the victim's chest and face." Belinda held up a small plastics bag which contained a hand written note that began with the follow.

To know my first name take it back to 1611. My first name ordered me to write my last name and age in it, this is the first clue.

"Do you get it now?" Leroy pushed his chair back from the table, closed his eyes and laid his head back from his chest and slowly opened his eyes. "Who else has seen this note?"

"Just the Captain and K.T."

"Are the scenes secured?"

"Yes, the first one Rodney Bell."

"Prints?"

"No!"

"Anything off the note?"

"None, he used paper from the apartment, said he's going on a killing spree in and around

Mecklenburg once we got off our lazy no good tails and get on point."

"Did he give any clue on when he might strike again?" Belinda hesitated. "He said he's waiting for you. Said that your career as a cop is suspect and that he's determine to prove to the people of this city that you are still that same old crooked S.O.B that you was sixteen years ago, so what is up with that? Do you think you may know this guy?" Leroy didn't answer.

"K.T. was the one who show it to me. I didn't know the reports were on my desk until after the second murder. Hell I been so backed up, by that time it really didn't matter. The next day we got another note in the mail. That's when we knew we had a Ted Bundy from the ghetto on our hands, and he is getting impatient with us."

"A repeater who actually leaves a bible at every scene, what he makes his victims have bible services first before he kills them?"

"Why are the ducks in the water today daddy? Don't they like playing in the grass?" Leroy and his daughter watched the ducks as they sat on the park bench. The beautiful all white ducks pedaled their little yellow feet back and forth across the water. Leroy watch but his mind was on the two murdered black men that were found dead in their homes. "What's up daddy?" she said. "What sugar cakes?"

"Why aren't they playing in the grass?" she asked impatiently. "Oh, they probably were playing in the grass earlier and got dirty so now they need a bath." the answer satisfied Kametica who continued to watch the ducks from the park bench. "Can I go feed the ducks now daddy?"

"Yes baby cakes but don't get to close."

"Okay daddy I won't," she said as she skipped across the park. She held the crackers tightly in her little hands. Leroy moved with her watching as she threw crackers into the water. He thought about the killer. How did he know about his days as a street hustle? Well that wouldn't have been too hard to find out. All he had to do was ask some of these old coons and they would have been like, '*Oh, Leroy that dude used to have Mecklenburg on lock.*'

"Why aren't they eating daddy?"

"Huh?"

"The ducks daddy, why aren't they eating?" she pointed. "That's because they don't want to get real fat like your Aunt Bridget." he hoped that she wouldn't go back and tell her aunt what he said. "Are the ducks on a diet daddy?"

"No I don't think so." he kneeled down and stroked Kametica's long braided hair and then hugged her. He looked into her brown eyes "let's call mommy and tell her we are on our way home. How does that sound?" Kametica ran across the parking lot and stopped when the sun hit her eyes. She turned around and waited for her father to catch up. Leroy put on his sunglasses, and grabbed her hand. "I have a big surprise for you... you'll see."

Burger King is on the left hand side coming off Hwy 74 across from McDonalds in Mecklenburg, a place where parents could still take their kids for a hamburger. Leroy lifted his daughter up into his arms and stood behind a gentleman in line. "Can I take your order please?" Leroy walked off from behind the gentleman and went to the lady at the second cash register. "Yes let me get a… hey! Girl I didn't know that you worked here. What's been going on?"

"Nothing much just chilling," Lisa Carson said as she leaned over to peck Kametica's cheek. "Well let me get a kid's meal with chicken tenders with a coke."

"Okay, hey are you still going with that girl from Shelby?" Leroy looked into Lisa's sexy face which showed the same bright brown eyes, and light complexion like her sister April, Kametica's mother. Lisa was thirty one and worked at Burger King full time. She was going to school at night but was arrested for possession of stolen goods on school grounds. The job at Burger King helps her make a little bit of money to flip and make ends meet. "Nah," Leroy answered. he started to give her a ten dollar bill Lisa waved it away. "Don't worry about it I gotcha."

"Thanks." Leroy put Kametica on the floor and grabbed his cell phone. A white lady at a table was giving him a nasty perverted look that made him sick to his stomach. Leroy noticed a chill in April's voice. She told him that Belinda called "Did she say what she wanted?" he tried to sound unconcerned. "Only that she wanted to know if you read the material that she gave you yet. She also said that she is glad that your back, what the hell is going on Leroy? I thought you…" "Well they asked big daddy to come back," he said smiling. "Why did you not tell me this when you came and picked up Kametica today?" at the drink machine Kametica giggled and slapped Lisa on the leg. "Officially I'll be on the job but I won't be reporting to the office. They may say I am still out. It's something I worked out with Belinda," he paused and added. "That will give me a couple of weeks to investigate a few cases before …" he cut himself off. "Tell you about it later."

"What about the Captain?"

"For the time being we will just avoid each other."

"I was getting used to you spending a lot of time at home, especially with me and Kametica." Leroy didn't say anything. "Where are you right now?"

"At Burger King, we just came back from the park," he said. "Kametica wanted to know why the ducks wouldn't come out of the water."

"What did you tell her?"

"I told her it was because they had been playing in the grass all morning and decided they needed to take a bath." she laughed. "Boy you stupid!"

"We had a good time today." Leroy said. "Tomorrow I have to work."

"Why, tomorrow is Labor Day."

"I have to go over some stuff and I need to see Chad Hunt tomorrow too." they were both silent. "We'll talk more about it later alright."

"Well, okay bye." without hesitating Leroy immediately called Belinda.

A soft sexy voice answered the phone. "Homicide, this is Lieutenant Bright."

"Belinda its Leroy I want to check out the Bell apartment, is it available?"

"It's locked but I have the keys here."

"Good, send it over tonight."

"Okay anything else?"

"What makes you think there's something else?"

"There is always something else."

"Well not this time," Leroy said. Actually there was but he wasn't going to give Belinda the satisfaction to rub it in his face. "I will be busy all day tomorrow so I will call you on Wednesday." Leroy hung up and went over to where his daughter was still playing with Lisa. "It's time to burn the road up your mom is expecting us."

"Where's my surprise?" Kametica asked. "What surprise?"

"Come on daddy!"

"Oh," Leroy glanced at the untouched ten dollar bill and pointed at the cash register. "There you go get it." Kametica's eyes lit up and she ran to the cash register. "Thanks daddy!" she said as she ran back over to hug him.

Chapter 2

The players club in west Charlotte is known for its hood like style, with its big bootie shaking women and out of control niggaz. The club was packed and the music was loud. People were dancing all over the place. Fat boy glanced down at the dance floor as he lowered his left hand down gripping his groaning. "Man that girl is thick." he muttered to himself. A short black lady dressed in tight white jeans with a red see through blouse walked across the dance floor. He recognized her immediately. "Hey Kim!" he shouted. "Your nigga Pacman is here."

"Where at?" she shouted back. "Over there at the bar follow me." her round phat ass and wide hips swayed deliberately as she journeyed through the crowded dance floor. Her high derriere sashayed with each step, with a well-timed flick of her hand she swept her straight black weave over her shoulder where it hung down to her thin waist.

Fat boy couldn't resist looking at her as they walked. He struggles not to disrespect his homeboy. He keeps his composure as he watches every eye in their path catch her arrival. Niggaz leered discretely although few were caught by their girl-friends and wives as they stopped in mid-drink to stare and found they couldn't tear their eyes away. Pacman watched the ladies dance, it aroused him. He stood up when she reached the bar, put his arms around her and his hands on her ass. He kissed her once on the lips. Fat boy greeted him and then headed back to the dance floor. "Girl you look good as hell tonight," said Pacman. "Thank you sweetie, those pants look really good on you. Are those the same ones you got in Shelby last week?"

"Yep."

"Nice pick Romeo," she said. Pacman grinned widely keeping his mouth closed tight even though he could barely keep himself from laughing out loud. She adored his smile. She thought it made him look sexy. It enhanced his strong features, his broad nose, big brown eyes, and dark skin.

"So what's up? How did the interview go? Did you get the promotion?" Pacman ignored her questions. She shook her head and reached in her purse and pulled out a blunt. "*Alright nigga two can play that game*," she thought to herself. She placed the blunt between her lips. Exaggerating every move so he was sure to see it, a light skin guy came over and offered her a light. Pacman waved him away hatefully almost hitting him over the head with his beer bottle. She lit her blunt with a thin gold lighter, she exhaled and let the thick smoke curled slowly upward past her eyes and hair as if she had all the time in the world. She purposely strained her breast against the red satin bodice. Pacman inhaled so deeply that almost no smoke escaped from his mouth when he exhaled. They watched each other silently until neither could contain it any longer and they both busted out laughing at the same time. "You are now looking at the new supervisor at Foothills in Mecklenburg," he said. "Oh baby you got the job! I am so happy for you."

Pacman's move up to supervisor had been well over due for some time now. Five years of kissing Mr. Charley's ass, and moving and unloading boxes on forklifts had finally paid off.

He enjoyed working at Foothills. He strode through the plant facility as if he owned the place, cutting deals with young dope dealers who wanted to set up shop underneath the warehouse where he worked, mostly teenage boys who didn't mind hitting him off a piece of whatever they had. Whether it was crack, weed, pills etc. He took it, but in the case of several well respected dealers a small offer is not an option. He did whatever it took to make a hustle. He made up his mind that he'll never be known as a broke ass nigga who sleeps on the streets. He remembered being on the block watching guys make that fast money. Oh yell the money, he wanted it! He needed it! It was all so far from the helpless days of his youth. As they both got through smoking their blunt he leaned over and whispered in Kim's ear. "I have a hard black magic stick for you." he licked her ear with the tip of his tongue. She giggled and touched his face. "I know baby," she said softly. "It's going to be perfect." she ran her fingers across his lips. "I can't wait until I get you home tonight so we can really work magic." he grinned at her. "Why wait?" he moved his hand slowly underneath the bar exploring her thigh with his fingers. Her body tingled as he rubbed his hand above her waist line, slipping his fingers down between her soft skin and white pants. His hand moved down until he felt wisps of moist hair. She shook. "Let's go home baby," she whispered as she unzipped his pants and handled him with exaggerated frisky strokes. "I have something real special for you when we get outside," she said. She laughed playfully as they both headed out the club.

Chapter 3

A yellowish white light reflected off the apartment buildings on Seitz Drive into Leroy and April's kitchen window. They sat facing each other across a round table. All that remained on the table after supper was a couple pieces of chicken, a Bud Light, and a bottle of Smirnoff. Moments before they had tucked Kametica into bed with a large stuffed puppy named Sappy, leaving the bedroom door slightly opened. The house was just one of the dozen on Seitz Drive across from the Food Lion supermarket that had been rehabilitated by urban entrepreneurs who found their investment increase fourfold over the past six years. In the case of Leroy and April however, it was not so much a desire to corner the real estate market, but a wish to find affordable housing that satisfied the districts residency requirements for Leroy's job. For April it held the advantage of a five block walk to her job as a secretary at William and Hart Corporation.

Like many couples Leroy and April were not married, nor were they girlfriend or boyfriend. They were more like sex room mates who just happen to have a child together. Even after sixteen years of knowing each other Leroy still flirts with April. Her skin was smooth, her lips full and juicy. She recently changed her hair style, and when she came home from the salon, Leroy would throw her on the bed and tell her that she looked like one of those hip-hop girls in a Lil Wayne video. He softly kissed between her perfectly round breasts. Leroy wasn't overly muscular but his chest and thighs were hard from lifting weights four times a week. His stomach was ripped, with a "full size black snake in his pants as April would call it. He just turned thirty-six but had a body of a man in his late twenties.

She lifted the bottle of Smirnoff to her lips and then put it down without drinking it. "What's up? Talk to me." Leroy told her about his conversation with Belinda and why he will not go back to work for another week or so. If he did the killer may try to strike again. A week and a half would buy time. He made it a rule not to keep April in the dark from his work. Many detectives never tell the people their close to about their jobs, always keeping things to themselves and playing the American hero. Although he didn't bring home the day to day urban nightmares. Leroy let her in on the hot cases or those of particular interest. He found April a good sounding board for his theories and ideas, she supplied an outside perspective. Sitting across from her he told her about the reports. "According to the report sheets the victims were either shot or stabbed. The first victim, a black male named Rodney Reuben Bell, age twenty five. Police were called to the apartment by the victim's sister. She told the police that she hasn't seen or heard from her brother in five days and she was concerned. Police found the victim lying in the bathroom with a red bible lying beside him. He was nude and his clothes in the sink. He had funny looking blue drawing on his arms and legs, with little written

bible phases all over the walls which were written in the

victim's own blood, No evidence of it being gang relate,

one of the detectives that were at the scene described

his head as a beach ball that had been stepped on. The

exact cause of death was listed as a blow to the head

by a blunt object, although he was stabbed ten times.

From the splatter patterns on the floor, technicians

determine that the stab wounds were administered ante

and post mortem. The killer stabbed, hit, and then

stabbed some more. Vacuum sweepings revealed no

foreign fibers, and the only hairs found at the scene

belonged to the victim. Detectives saw no signs of a

break in."

"How do you think he got in?" she asked.

"I don't know, either he knew the killer or he

talked his way in. I need to hurry and get down there

and take a look around myself."

"Why the hurry?" she asked confusedly? "The landlord is tripping out, he's ordering the apartment to be cleaned by tomorrow evening, and the detectives didn't tell him not to clean it just yet, said he didn't want this mess hurting his rental status. Those were his exact words." April heard the owner in her mind and shivered. She was a student at East Rutherford High School. Her family is from Spindale North Carolina. Her father works at United Southern and her mother worked for D.O.C. Although these stories didn't bother her the way they had when he first joined the department, she could only take a little at a time. She pictured the man just lying on the floor, the stab wounds, the blood... She felt herself starting to lose her mind. Without a word she got up and went over to the refrigerator and grabbed herself another Smirnoff. She took a sip and forced a smile. All she wanted was a drink. Then she told him to continue. "The second murder was almost a carbon copy of the first. The victim's name is Robert Lee Maxwell. This time a note was left," he recited it from memory including the part about him. "Wow! This isn't like your other cases Leroy. Are you sure the killer mentioned you in the note?"

"Yep," he lean forward and pressed a hand on April's arm and caressed the side of her hand. "Everything is going to be alright, don't sweat it. So why don't you just go to bed, I'll be there in a minute," he said. She got up and walked into the bathroom to take a piss, and then she went upstairs to the bedroom. Leroy sat and looked out the window at the Food-Lion supermarket across the street. "Son of a bitch!" he muttered. About an hour and a half later he slipped into bed and nestled his chest against April's back, feeling her heat. They lay there together, eyes still open trying to get the images out of his head so he could go to sleep.

Chapter 4

Leroy woke at twenty-five minutes after eight, brushed his teeth and had a glass of milk. He let April sleep. It took him ten minutes to reach the Mecklenburg Prison Camp; a three acre, two building complex on Camp Road about nine miles away. Leroy had phoned the Superintendent Chad Hunt yesterday and said he'd be coming by. Hunt was ready when he arrived. Hunt usually didn't work on Labor Day but made a special trip to meet Leroy. He wore a light brown three piece suit. His yellow shirt appeared heavily starched. "I take it this is a business meeting," he said. "Yes business," Leroy said. He effect an air of solemnity that he knew would please Hunt. "Okay, I will have the inmate brought in," he sent orders into his intercom a then sat back in his large leather chair. "He'll be here in a minute, until he gets here I need to talk to you Mr. Johnson off the record if you don't mine."

"Sure."

"As a Mecklenburg police officer now you have a right to request any prisoner for questioning. I would not deny you that right, but I can do that you know just for the simple fact that you have done time here before."

"Yes, but Governor Easley granted me immunity. So my past is no longer a factor in this matter." Leroy knew damn well that Hunt couldn't deny him permission to question a prisoner. But he could damn sure make it difficult. Standard procedure called for prisoners to be brought to the Mecklenburg County Jail by county officers. Hunt has bent the rules before and allowed Leroy to take custody directly from the prison and bring the inmate back to Mecklenburg himself. It was part of a payback. Back in Leroy's street days Hunt's teenage son C.J. bought an ounce of crack from one of Leroy's homeboys. Leroy recognized the boy's face and whisked him away from the scene, tossed the crack into the woods and drove him home. The incident was never spoken of again. Hunt continued. "I know you wouldn't abuse your position."

"I wouldn't do that," Leroy said. "You must keep in mind that Tyrone is still my responsibility."

"I understand," Leroy replied. A voice on the intercom alerted him that Tyrone had arrived in front of the office hallway. "Tell them to wait a minute," he said into the box. "My officers have told me that for the past nine days after seeing you he's not slept well, I insisted that he needed to see a psychiatrist. The doctor told me on the low that Tyrone has nightmares about the…" Leroy started to say something but Hunt held up his hand. "Let me finish," he said sternly. "I'm glad that your reasons to visit are legitimate and that Tyrone doesn't mind. His lawyer even signs off on it, I've done my job." Hunt rocked forward and paused staring Leroy in the eye. "What I'm saying is be careful, even though I'm legally protected, if something were to happen to him because of visits during non-visiting periods it wouldn't look good for me or Raleigh." the walls rang with the words. "Do I make myself clear?"

"Gotcha," Leroy said. Hunt took a deep breath and rocked his chair backward. "Alright then we understand each other," he turned to the intercom. "Send the prisoner in."

Chapter 5

Leroy peeled the yellow crime scene tape off the door knob, rolled it between his hands and tossed the tacky ball in a nearby bush. He unlocked the door and swung it open. A rush of rotting smelling breeze hit his nose. "God-damn!" he said as he took a step backward out the front door trying to regain his composure. His eyes watered. Once inside he stood motionless in the living room. He's dealt with smelling death many times before by centering himself mentally and breathing only snippets of air slowly, he increased the amount deeper and deeper until he breathed normally. His mind flashed back on the murder of an eight year old girl in Ellenboro four years ago whose body went undiscovered for days. The officers wouldn't enter the bathroom so Leroy went in first. When the hot decayed air hit him he sped back into the living room with his hand covering his mouth and nose. He found an old newspaper laying in the corner of the floor, he reached into his pocket and pulled out his lighter. He lit the paper and went back into the bathroom while waving the smoking newspaper back and forth until the smoke neutralized the odor. Black magnetic fingerprint dust covered almost every surface of the man's apartment. Blood splatters and bloody bible verses could be seen on the walls, doors, and floors. Leroy looked down and founded himself standing on an outline drawn in chalk. He snapped on a set of latex gloves. The apartment masculine nature struck him immediately; the medicine cabinet was filled with razors, shaving cream, and condoms. A large picture of nude white girls hung on the wall. A dozen of hustler magazines were stacked beneath the bathroom sink cabinet. He added this to the victim's profile, "*A pervert,*" Leroy scanned the bath tub. A soap dish laid inside the tub with a wash rag placed neatly on top of the shower curtain. The bedroom yields nothing in particular other than its hard gangster like style nature that struck Leroy. Marijuana drapes covered the window, and below it a few vibe magazines laid on the radiator cover. A photo showed the man and three other guys holding up guns with red scarves hanging from the right side of their back pockets. The kitchen shelves were fully stocked with corn flakes and can foods. Leftover pig's feet and chitins in plastic containers filed the refrigerator. "*Obviously this guy wasn't Muslim."* add it to the list, for all the damn good it would do. This guy killer wouldn't be found by exploring his lifestyle. Any link would be found in evidence left behind, not whom he hung out with or where he bought his food. Leroy closed the refrigerator door and headed into the living room. He sat down in a chair and concentrated on the last few minutes in the life of Mr. Bell.

'There he is laying on the bathroom floor, life slipping away. Is he done stabbing him with blood on his hands? No, there was no blood on the note. The killer washes his hands first then grabs a sheet of paper, sits in the chair and writes the note. Finger prints on the chair and note? K.T. checked. Nothing! Folds it and puts it in the envelope. Licks and seals it, finds a stamp on the desk. K.T. checked it too, nothing. Does he look back before he leaves? He walks outside drops the letter in

the mail box, it's rained since then, prints washed away'

"Dammit, think nigga, think."

Chapter 6

The sun gleamed on Tina Walker, short with a sexy figure. She was dressed in a conservative pink suit which matched her shoes. She stood in front of the police headquarters staring uneasy at the camera. "Come on shit I don't have all day." as if they cared at all. The three technicians purposely took their time exaggerating every move as they set up lights and established the sound level in Walker's ear piece. J.J jerked a cord that caused Walker to cup her ear and yelp. "Sorry my bad, I think we're all set to go Walker." J.J and his partner Jabril smiled at each other over the prank. They knew Walker was not paying them any attention. She was too busy playing in her hair. All the technicians thought she wore a wig but they couldn't prove it. "Five, four, three, two and go!" J.J shouted. "Police investigators are looking for the person who beat and stabbed two Mecklenburg men during the past week. Although police will neither confirm nor deny it, sources tell Eyewitness News that investigators believe the murders are the work of one person, with me now is Mecklenburg police Captain David Cox. Captain can you shed some light on what we been hearing. Is the department indeed searching for a serial killer? Who struck down two men in the Dodge City area?" Cox didn't want to be talking to no reporters but the Chief needed someone from the department to represent. When the reporters came out Cox's orders were clear. "Put on your best face and make no comments about the murders."

"Yes! We are presently conducting investigations into the murders of two men in the Dodge City area.

The cases are two of many ongoing homicides being investigated by the MCPD."

"Captain," Walker said. We been told by people in your own department that similar clues were found at each crime scene leading them to believe the murders were the work of one man. How do you respond to that?"

"I can't comment on specific crime scene evidence while an investigation is underway."

"If this is indeed true about similar evidence at each site wouldn't that indicate that we have a serial killer?" Cox lost his cool, blood vessels in his eyes filled red. "I'd like to talk to the people who told you that, maybe they know more about the case than I do," he said sarcastically. Walker ignored the comment. "Captain in light of all this, isn't it possible that this was the work of one individual and that he could kill again?"

"It's possible, we will just have to wait and see what happens." Mrs. Walker took a few steps to her right leaving Cox standing alone away from the camera. Cox felt a little stupid and didn't know what to do except fall back a few steps. He didn't know whether to leave or just stay. J.J walked over to him and said. "We appreciate you coming out, that will be all Sir."

"So there you have it," said Walker looking straight into the camera. "It's possible according to Captain Cox that the city is being stalked by a serial killer who as we know of has killed two young men and could strike again before he's caught. We'll be following this story giving you live details as they develop. Pam Anderson back to you."

"And cut!" said Jabril. Walker exhaled heavily dropping her head into her chest and her hand with the microphone fell to her side exhaustedly like she had been running for days. As J.J and Jabril remove the equipment Walker saw Cox arguing on the phone. The person on the phone must have been someone he thinks is leaking information about the cases. Walker thought, she went to the back door of the van and stuck her head inside. "How was I?"

"You were great Tina," J.J said.

"Thank you," added Tina.

"You really put Cox out on blast about the leaks in the department. Hey just between you and me, did a cop really give you all that info or were you just fronting?"

"Sorry boys a woman never tells her secrets but I'll tell you one thing this is the biggest story that ever hit Mecklenburg and nobody knows what I know. So I am going to ride this all the way to the bank."

Chapter 7

The white and blue Ford Mustang spited out dark exhaust as it waddled along in the fast lane of the highway. The speed limit on Hwy 74 was 55. Its driver and passenger were content to do eighty miles per hour, while B.M.Ws, Hummers, and other thorough breeds in the slow lane refused to let their speedometer clock over 50. The driver Mario Jackson and Curtis Murchison the passenger road comfortably with their seats tilted back and the music jumping. "Damn that's my shit! Turn that up," shouted Mario. "I gotcha' my nigga," replied Curtis as he reached to turn up the volume. Leroy pulled up behind the mustang at the intersection across from the Bank of America, catching his eye with a blink of lights in the side mirror. "Oh shit! 5-0," blurted Mario. "Well speed up nigga you know I am dirty as hell," said Curtis. "Just chill I got this," replied Mario. "*Stay calm,*" Mario thought to himself. He pulled over to the right side of the road and put the mustang in park allowing the engine to run. Leroy steps out of his black Ford Crown Vick and walks over to the driver side of the mustang with his gun drawled. "Freeze nigga!" he shouted playfully.

"Damn what the fuck?" he recognized who it was. "C'mon dude, don't scare me like that what the hell is wrong with you? You know my heart isn't that good," said Mario who had triple bypass surgery four years ago. Who used untaxed dope money to pay what the insurance didn't cover. "Why would you be scared? Is there dope in the car?" Leroy asked. "Hell nah," Curtis blurted out while trying to suitcase a ball of hard in his ass. "C'mon man stop tripping you know we go way back like George Jefferson's hair line." Mario is one of the few people left in Mecklenburg who grew up with Leroy. Ever since Leroy started working for the police department he has been looking out for Mario, giving him heads up on when the police were going to run in on him or when the feds are in town. "You know I'm just fucking with you my nigga. The reason I stopped you is that I needed to know how to get to Gomers," Leroy asked. "You mean the bootlegger spot next to New Hope?" Curtis asked in a curious manner. "Yup," replied Leroy. Mario leaned his right arm over the steering wheel with his head down, left hand rubbing across his forehead while he tries to think. "Go straight down this road and hit exit 221. Keep going till you reach the liquor store on Millers Avenue. Take a left on that road and go about five blocks and take a left on New Town Road. It's the second house on your right, you can't miss it."

"Good looking," Leroy said while giving Mario dap.

"If you don't mind me asking, why you need to go to Gomers for?"

"I need to talk to K.T. and I know his tail is down there on the card table giving his money away."

"I know that's right," said Mario while shifting his gear into drive. "I see you later," said Leroy as he headed back to his car. "Peace my nigga," Mario said as he pulled off.

"Who the fuck is knocking at my door like that," muttered Peanut as he raced to the back door. "Who is it?"

"It's me Leroy Johnson."

"Man why in the hell are you knocking at my door like the police?" asked Peanut. "Fool I am the police where is K.T."

"He's in the back." Leroy spotted K.T. distinctive lucky visor in the corner of the back room. K.T. had worn it religiously since dealt a royal flush during a game six months ago winning about eight thousand dollars. It wasn't a coincidence that he had asked for the day off. He needed the money bad. "He's busy," said Peanut. "Tell him I need to see him a.s.a.p."

"No can do Leroy, privacy is what I am selling you know that. Away from nagging old ladies and broke ass niggaz," he said it like a corporate slogan. "Now Peanut aren't you on the run now don't let me have to..."

"Okay I get the point, KELLY!" he called out to the table. Nobody looked up. "KELLY!" he repeated. Kelly Thompson heard his name but ignored it. He was more interested in working his way to the pot with three kings and a guarded smile. Even with the smile he couldn't beat Fred's three aces and two jacks. "Man the hell with this I'm out!" he said as he threw down his cards. He stood up and walked out the room cussing. "What the hell do you want?"

"There," he said pointing to Leroy who was keeping pace next to the back door. "It's my day off so what the hell do you want Leroy?"

"I wanted to see your Barack Obama looking ass in person, where is your truck?"

"Out back why?"

"I need you to go somewhere with me."

"I'm for real this better be important." Despite his shit talking it didn't take much for Leroy to drag K.T. from the bootlegger. K.T's visor seemed to be losing its value and he wasn't ready to call it quits. "You owe me Leroy." K.T is the straight up type and will tell you like it is. He has more confidence than anyone else in the department. His specialty was the private lab jobs and his favorite drink is E&J even though he hasn't had a taste in months. Leroy was waiting for him at Route 221 exit. "Now, what is so damn important that it couldn't wait?" K.T. asked. After Leroy filled him in "I went through that apartment four times and didn't find nothing but I got a feeling let's bounce. I'll drive you back to your truck later," said Leroy.

On the way downtown K.T. thought a change in liquor may do him some good, from E&J to Hessney. Belinda met them in the lab, she was carrying a plastic evidence bag from the Bell man's apartment. "Cox was on television," she said. "Did you see him?" neither of the men answered. "He was talking to that big nose news lady Walker, she told him she knew we had a repeater."

"Nobody knows about that but me, you two, and Cox."

"How do you think she knew? Do you think that Cox told her?" asked Leroy. "Yeah right picture that," K.T. laughed as he poured himself another cup of

Hessney. "Have some?" K.T. never worried about anyone snitching on him to the man about his drinking on the job. He felt safe and comfortable in his lab. He could laugh and drink all he wanted. "What exactly did Walker say?" Leroy asked. "That a cop told her that the same evidence was left at each site."

"What the Bible?"

"She didn't say but that's the only thing it could be."

"Well maybe she doesn't know anything Belinda, maybe she was just telling a story."

"Could be but I don't like leaks. I know it didn't come from you or K.T which leaves the Captain." as Belinda began walking out she added. "Keep me informed I've got to go and check out some things." K.T. put down his bottle snapped on latex gloves and reached into the evidence bag and looked at Leroy.

"Okay man what is your big feeling?"

"Kill the lights and get the laser," said Leroy. A

few minutes later K.T. and Leroy leaned over the black

lab table. The only light in the room came from a

diffused red laser crisscrossing an area on the

envelope that had been delicately pried open with a

razor knife. Moments before K.T. had seesawed the

blade back and forth using measured strokes. A

technique learned from watching C.S.I Miami. The

fumes made Leroy cough. "We don't need much DNA,"

said K.T. That's deoxyribonucleic acid" he added

quickly."

"Man I know what DNA is, I watch C.S.I."

K.T. didn't respond as he continued to

reposition the laser over the yellow envelope mailed by

the killer. "Nothing," he said. "I guess he didn't cut

himself when he licked it like you thought."

"Wait a second, have you ever gotten a paper

cut? You don't always bleed, sometimes the skin just

separates. The cut is so sharp it just closes back up

immediately," Leroy said. "Still hurts like shit," said K.T.

"Exactly, there's a chance we can find some skin cells

sliced from his tongue." K.T. did a double take. "Where

did you learn that from?"

"Told you, I've be checking out that C.S.I. stuff

so keep looking, I'm going to call Cell Core." when he

returned .K.T. was sitting at his desk, the envelope now

cut in half. He laid one piece in a plastic bag dated and

labeled <u>Bell Envelope-Half</u>. The other piece was also in

a bag and labeled <u>Cell Core</u> along with a few sheets of

paper informing their scientist about the samples

condition, case number and other information. "They're

ready for us," said Leroy as he took his keys out of his

pocket. "Going to be high and Belinda is going to be mad if we don't find anything here."

"Let me worry about Belinda. Let's just get the hell out of here." K.T. put the plastic bag in a manila envelope and tape it shut. He filled out a form taking responsibly for evidence and signed it. As they were getting on the elevator they bumped into Belinda. "Where are you two knuckle heads going?"

"To Caroleen."

"Why?"

"Cell Core."

"Okay what's going on?" after a short conversation, emphasized by lots of hand going in lots of directions K.T. and Leroy finally made it into the parking lot. "Wait a second!" Belinda screamed after them. "I almost forgot why I came back --- here Leroy," she said as she gave Leroy the cell phone he requested. K.T. was already in the car and couldn't hear them. "Don't make me look stupid Leroy. This DNA stuff is high and I've got to justify each request." Leroy searched for a smart ass remark to say but couldn't think of one. "Don't sweat it," Leroy hesitated. "What did Cox say about the leak to the TV lady today?"

"He said he didn't know where it came from."

"You believe that?"

"I don't know who to believe anymore Leroy for real, I'm just getting tired of the bullshit, just don't screw up alright." as Leroy got in the car K.T. turn to Leroy and said "Didn't think she'd fall for it."

"Had too, it's the only thing we have, look she even gave me a cell phone."

"Wow she must like you," said K.T. Homicide detectives used extra cell phones for private calls or calls they didn't want coming through the office like booty calls. Leroy wanted it both so he could separate his work from his private life. "Have you spoken to Cox lately?"

"I don't mess with that dude anymore. We communicate by memos, he writes them and I ignore them."

"I'm like you I don't like that muthafucka either," K.T .said. As they pulled into traffic Cell Core diagnostics was housed in a large brick building in a copper industrial area, which stood in front of an old furniture warehouse. Head scientist Amanda Rose met them. Leroy stuck out his hand "What's up Amanda good to see you again. This is Kelly Thompson from our department." Amanda Rose's lab coat didn't allow for imaginative thoughts about her shape. K.T. shook her hand, the goggles hanging from her neck didn't add to the hard on either. But it didn't matter to Amanda she was a straight up lesbian. Under her supervision Cell Core had grown from a small Charlotte base to a multimillion dollar industry, based on the most basic chemical structure unique to each person DNA, the chances of two people having the same DNA was one in a million. Most DNA typing is used for paternity testing for a child support cases, but law enforcement was learning its value in homicide and rape cases. Semen, skin, blood and saliva all contain DNA. "Nice to meet you Kelly, what do we have?" Leroy couldn't describe the case in detail because if it went to court Cell Core could only testify on what they had done and not assumptions about anything else. The less they knew the better. Leroy told her he wanted DNA extracted from the envelope and typed. As they walked into the lab room people hustled in and out excusing themselves as they hung up lab coats, placing eyewear on racks, and throwing away their gloves. Each person worked in a separate area on his or her own project. To keep the chain of evidence intact, the company insisted one scientist work a case from beginning to end. Rose planned to handle this one herself. "I have a feeling there may be skin cells from a tongue in the saliva," said Leroy.

"Did you look for blood?"

"I did, KT answered. "No blood, but I did see some caked liquid probably mixed up glue and saliva from the envelope," he said

"And you have the other half of the envelope?"

"Yup." Amanda talked as she filled out a receipt. "Okay I'll get right on it as soon as you leave, I don't know if we have enough material to work with. If not I will need the other part of the envelope. I'll give you a call in a few days to let you know." Amanda

disappeared into the lab shaking her head as she went.

"Nice looking woman," K.T. said as they left the

building. "Thick too, wouldn't mind hitting that," he

muttered. "What did you say?" Leroy asked. "Nothing

man, just take me back to my truck."

Chapter 8

The knock on the screen door woke April up

from her nap. As she struggled to her feet she

saw Kametica race into her bedroom.

 "Who is that at the door?"

"It's Belinda mom," Kametica said.

"Alright go let her in and get daddy." Belinda

known Kametica since she was a little baby. She

was even given the honor to be her god mother.

"I guess Leroy has told you what's been going on," Belinda said to April.

"Of course Belinda Leroy never keeps anything from me."

"I guess that's only right for him to do so." Belinda walked around the living room studying the photos of Leroy and his little girl. She turned back to April.

"Wish I had my little boy living with me --- we would --- she shrugged. April knew the story. Before becoming a lieutenant Belinda worked long hours and started drinking too much and tooting powder. She let her private life get the best of her which at the end cost her, a loving husband and son.

"When was the last time you seen your son Chris? I bet he is big as hell, how old is he now?"

"Fifteen, his father moved him to New York to be near relatives about two years ago, haven't seen him in more than a year and a half. His daddy is supposed to bring him down for Christmas." Belinda has always had feelings for Leroy but couldn't imagine sleeping with him do to her friendship with April. Once on a stake out when they were alone, just talking and shooting the shit Leroy confided. "Belinda when is you going to let me hit that nobody is going to know. I'm just going to keep it real with you. I have never mess with a white girl in my life. My mother told me that if I ever bought a white girl to her house she will kill me. That has stuck with me ever since."

Leroy walked into the living room as April was about to say something. She checked herself. "I've got to go," she said. "I will see you later Belinda." when April was out of ear shot Belinda spoke. "He knows your back, here's another note," she held it out. Leroy took the note and read it silently. *'Now that your back I can start back killing, thank you Detective Leroy Johnson.'*

"A week in a half, I thought I had a week and a half," Leroy said. "Who told him God Dammit, Who...!"

Leroy flipped. "Leroy chill out."

"Don't tell me to fucking chill out Belinda, what the hell is going on here? He knows my every move better than I do. How does he know? Nobody knows but I bet it's that bitch ass nigga Cox I'm going to beat his black ass."

"Don't do that Leroy please wait." Leroy grabbed his coat. April heard the yelling and came in just as Leroy slammed the door. "It's my fault April," was all Belinda could say as she chased after Leroy.

Chapter 9

Leroy's growing dislike for the department was starting to show. He started to wonder if he had made a big mistake by becoming the black cop that KRS-1 rapped about back in the day, fifteen years previously when he was released from the Department of Correctional for a crime he didn't do. He received thirty thousand dollars for compensation from the state. Money that he could have used to start up a small business, but instead he used some of the money to have his record cleared and the rest of it for college. His major was criminology and he minored in psychology. He impressed the recruits in his home district so much that they practically begged him to join. So after a week of thinking about it, he thought. *"What the hell, I can be the black Vick Mackey of Mecklenburg."*

"I've been expecting you Leroy." Cox sat behind a black desk almost every inch of the walls shouted with shoulder patches from other police departments, citations, and photos of Cox shaking hands with supposedly black leaders, such as Jesse Jackson and Al Sharpton. Framed pictures of the Governor and police chief hung behind his head. "Belinda called and said you were still pissed off. Hell, I gave you your job back and you had a lot of time to spend with your family, so what the hell is your problem?" Leroy used all of his energy just to keep from reaching over the desk and smacking the shit out of Cox. "Not only does that news woman know about our investigation, the killer knows I'm back on the job."

"I see, Is that all you have to say? C'mon man."

"C'mon hell, there is a blabber mouth and I think that blabber mouth is you. I think you let it slip at one of those lodge meetings or maybe at the club to one of your boyfriends you've been seeing."

"You need to watch your damn mouth!" Cox shouted. "You are forgetting who the hell you are talking to Detective?" Cox returned calm and that only infuriated Leroy more. The phone rang and as Cox reached for it Leroy clamped his hand over it. "Hold up we are not done talking."

"Nigga have you lost your mind? You better remove your hand from my phone." Leroy jerked his arm away. "You're good, you may even be the best we have but I'm not going to continue

putting up with your shit. You are replaceable,

don't ever forget that and another thing," Cox's

voice boomed. "I am the one catching hell from

Mr. Charley. Do you think I like the chief asking

me about what's being said in the media about

this investigation? What am I supposed to say?

Oh yes master Sir, I got my best nigga looking

into it. But what I really got is an asshole

snooping around with nothing to show for it. But I

have to use him because the killer and he are

butt buddies. Yes master Sir, he even writes him

love letters. You know the one Sir, the one who

has been in the penitentiary." Leroy slammed his

hands on the desk and looked Cox in the eye.

"Tell me the damn truth did you tell anyone

about the bibles? Did you say we have a

repeater? Oh yeah and one more thing how

does the killer know I'm back to work?" Cox smacked his lips. "Hell I don't know Detective and I don't have to explain myself. It seems that you have forgotten that I am the Captain and you're the detective, this is your investigation and not mine, unless you can't handle the job. I suggest you look at your crazy ass friend. What's his name Thompson? I heard that he will do anything for a rock." Leroy cocked his arm, fist closed. Cox stood up and braced. The door flung open. "Well I'm glad to see that you two are finally getting along," said Belinda. Leroy ignored the comment. Cox sat down. "Yeah we're getting along just fine," Cox said. "Now that we're all here it seems a good time to discuss our case." Both Cox and Leroy were glad to see that Belinda had interrupted when she did. "We have a problem Captain, actually we have a few problems. For one the killer knows our every move, or at least he knows Leroy's every move. Secondly someone has been leaking our information to the media." Leroy and Cox both glance at each other. "I think it's important that we resolve our internal differences and figure out how the information is getting out." Belinda waited for one of them to say something but neither did. "Well I'm convinced that no one in this room said anything." Leroy's eyes shot over at Cox. "I also trust K.T, I've known him for years." Cox returned the look. "So what do we do now?" Leroy asked. "I think that we need to tap Walker's phone, find out who's been calling her."

"Tap the media, oh hell no," Cox said. "You don't even know if that's how she is getting her information he added."

"Maybe she knows the killer," blurted Leroy. Cox tapped a pen at the bottom of his lip. "What if we're wrong then what? They'll fire the shit out of us if they find out, well except the white girl --- no offense," Cox said. "It seems that the almighty Captain Cox is scared of Mr. Charley."

"Fuck you Leroy, get the hell out both of you."

 "You just can't let it go can you Leroy," Belinda said as she was going out the door. "You just have to say something smart."

 "You're damn right especially when it's my black ass out there in the streets and not his."

Chapter 10

Leroy pulled in the parking lot entrance and waved as he normally does when he see a good looking female correction officer leaving

the prison entrance. The majority of females that

work at Mecklenburg Correctional were black

single mothers who barely make ends meet.

They would desperately do anything to have a

good man to treat them right. He nosed his car

into the handicapped parking spot which is one

of the advantages of being a cop. As Leroy

made his way inside he saw a fat black woman

clutching a baby wrapped in a blue blanket. The

woman couldn't have been no older than

nineteen. She wore tight blue jeans an all-white

t-shirt and black Reebok Classics. She glanced

up at Leroy as she pressed herself against the

wall to let him get by the narrow area between

herself and the crowd of people. She clutched

her hand over the baby's head as if Leroy was

going to grab the baby. He smiled at her but she

gave him a look as if she were saying *"nigga please."* she lifted the baby to her shoulder and walked out. Leroy looked around the room which was filled mostly with young black women who were there visiting their baby's daddy, boyfriend, or brother. He handed over his three-fifty seven to the red neck looking officer at the front desk who asked to see his badge. As he placed the gun under his desk he looked at Leroy again. "Hey I know you, Mr. Johnson if I'm not mistaken. Inmate turned police, I would like to know how in the hell..."

 "Cracker shut the fuck up," Leroy interrupted and then walked away making his way through the crowd to the visitation room. Leroy was led into a large room with about ten long tables lined up in a row with chairs stacked on top of each other in the corner. By the time he grabbed a chair to sit down a door opened and Tyrone walked in, he was a year older than Leroy. They shared the same features, slightly high cheek bones, large flat nose and a dark brown complexion. There was no doubt to anyone that they weren't brothers, his hair was nappy and his face was ashy dry. He sag his pants as if he were still a kid and dragging his feet as if he had one hundred pounds weights strap around his ankles. "What's up bro, doing okay?" Leroy asked. "I'm doing alright what about you?"

"I'm making it."

"That's what's up," Tyrone replied. Tyrone lit a Newport with one that was almost gone. "Damn bro I need some help."

"What in the hell have you done now?" asked Leroy. "I'm in debt bro."

"How much are you in for?"

"About almost twenty thousand dollars."

"Damn nigga! I don't have that type of money," said Leroy. "I know that bro but…" Tyrone leaned up closer to whisper something to him. "I know you can help me smuggle in a quarter Kilo. I can hustle that off and pay my debt and still have a lot of money left over." Leroy hesitated for a second before he spoke. "Well I'll see what I can do." Tyrone nodded. "Is Coco coming to see you?"

"Hell no --- you know how women are when it comes to messing with niggaz in prison, they feel that we are on their time. So I say fuck them hoes."

"You right," Leroy said with a smile. The conversation stopped. The pause was uncomfortable for both of them. Tyrone clasped his hands together, elbows on the table as if he was praying. He slowly tilted his head in between his arms with his eyes shut. "Shit," he said. "You alright man?"

"Dreams bro, I have been having dreams about what happened that night when she got...." Leroy held his hand. "Take it easy bro, it's Okay."

"Every night I have the same dreams. It feels like I am going crazy in this muthafucka bro." Tyrone tried to rub his fingers through his nappy head but they got stuck. "Just try not to think about it so much."

"I have been trying not to but..." his voice cracked. "Do you want to speak with Dr. Smith?"

"We have spoken before but that shit doesn't help."

"What can I do bro?"

"Get me out of here bro, please get me out."

Leroy placed his hand on his brother's shoulder.

"I'm trying bro, I'm trying."

Chapter 11

"Is everything straight?" Lewis asked. Pam Brown didn't respond. She lifted her red and white Hilfiger sweater over her head while he watched her large titties jiggle back and forth. She reaches on top of the coffee table and grabbed the remote. With a few tugs she pulled off her timberland boots then she finally responded to the question. "Yup, the brother is perfect."

"No trouble getting in?"

"Nope, it was easy." she began flicking stations on the TV set. She glanced at the pile of Hustler magazines on the sofa. "What the hell have you been doing?"

"Jacking off what do you think," replied Lewis. He reached under the pile and grabbed a particular magazine. "Check this one out." Pam took the magazine. A few pages fell out on the floor. "Disgusting, you gross nigga."

"Phat ass just the way I like it," she studied the pictures carefully and felt a twitch in between her legs. "I wonder what makes these dumb bitches pose for magazines like this."

"Hell money, a woman would do anything for money."

"Bullshit nigga, bullshit."

Chapter 12

"Do you read your Bible Mrs. Walker?" the voice on the phone sounded calm and deep. "What, who in the hell is this and how did you get my number?"

"I think you know who this is." Walker became frightened in her own home. She immediately jumped out of bed and ran to her son's bedroom, noticing that he was safe and sound asleep. Feeling frustrated and paranoid she searched through her house to make sure that whoever it was on the other end of the phone hasn't broken in, fear surged through her body and she could barely hold the phone steady. It wasn't so much the fear of talking to a psycho, but anxiety of this being the biggest story of her career. Her lips and mouth turned dry. "Tell me what the meaning behind the Bible is."

"I can make you famous Walker." Walker perceived the disembodied voice determined and in control. "Sure, sure we can help each other," Walker said. "I would like to hear your side of the story. I want to know more about the murders and—

"Yes the murders," said the voice on the phone. "You know they were only used to show them lazy ass polices that I can do their job better than them." the voice changed, it sound more challenging almost arrogate. "Well of course I know it was just to get them to do their job."

Walker was confused, she didn't know what this crazy man was talking about. "I would like to meet you," said Walker. "Get you on TV, I'll hide you in the cut, disguise your voice." no response. "Is that a deal?" ask Walker. Still no response. "Hello, hello?" the voice returned harsh. "No cameras, that is playing it too close right now maybe another time."

"Certainly whatever it's your call."

 "Do you know where the Spindale House is?"

"Of course I do," Walker Lied. She didn't know a damn thing about Spindale. "Five O'clock. Come alone."

"How will I know you?" the phone went dead. Walker was frozen, still gripping the phone listening to the buzz. When she hung up the phone she looked at her watch. 'Four O'clock, she went into her work room and grabbed her cell phone and google in the name. "Bingo, Spindale House."

<u>Chapter 13</u>

Mike Surratt couldn't ignore watching the white girls walking out the school house from across the street. At seventeen Mike has already been with almost every girl in his hood. Mike was very tall for his age, light skin with curly hair, the typical pretty boy type nigga. He was just released from training school a week ago for carrying a concealed weapon on school property. Mike stashed a half ounce of hard in a nearby bush behind his grandmother's house and ran across the street were cars and buses were pulling out from the school parking lot. The only thing in his mind was a piece of ass and a dub sack. He thought if he was lucky he may could hook up with one of those rich white girls and get his freak on. He felt his leg muscles burn as he sprinted in front and around a school bus going for the curb. He prepared himself as he stepped up to get his rap on but instead heard a female voice. "What's up cutie?" Mike turned and saw a sexy ass white girl behind the wheel, with a smile on his face Mike walked over to her car. "What's up with you sexy?" Mike replied. "Just heading home until I saw you, what's your name?"

"Mike, but my niggaz call me Gunn what's yours?"

"Eve but call me E."

"Well E what does a nigga have to do to get with a fine ass girl like you?"

"Well I don't know, I guess you will have to get in and find out."

"That's what I'm talking about," Mike replied. He opened the car door and hopped in. "Smoke weed?"

"Hell yeah I do."

"Do you know where we can get some?"

"I know a nigga in Dodge City that sell weed," Mike said. "Where's Dodge City?"

"Take a right here and go about ten blocks down this road. Then turn left and we will be in Dodge City. The niggaz house is the fifth one on the left," Mike folded his self in the leather seat. "You bang?"

"Yeah, why you ask?"

"I noticed a blue scarf hanging from your left pocket."

"I can tell you not new to the hood," Mike said. "How much do you need?"

"Just give me ten and I chip in the other half." Eve reached into her purse and grabbed a ten dollar bill and handed it to Mike. "I'll be right back." without hesitating Mike opened up the car door and jumped out, raced up a steep hill to a small brick house, and before he could knock, a short ugly black man slung the door open. "What the hell do you want young buck?" the man asked. "Let me get a dub sack," Mike asked. The man looked Mike up and down wondering if he could be trusted. "Alright wait here." the man turned around and eased into the back room, seconds later the man returned. "Here you go boy." Mike handed him two ten's and ran back down the hill to the car. "Did you get it?" "Yeah, let's bounce." as they both headed out of Dodge City they decided to pull behind an old super market that had been out of business for seven years. Eve idle the engine and watched Mike fiddle in his pocket for the weed. "I'll roll, let me have it," Eve said with one hand out while holding a philly cigar in the other. "Damn this smell like some fire."

"It is I smoked some of it the other day," Mike said. Eve reached into the bag spilling pieces of weed in between her legs. "Shit."

 "Here let me," Mike slid his hand down between her thick thighs, rubbing her pussy with the back of his fingertips. Eve tensed up allowing him to continue. "Damn that pussy is phat," said Mike. Eve reached over and unzipped Mike's pants pulling out his massive hard dick. Mike saw the wilderness in Eve's eyes as she wrapped her pink mouth around the head of his dick. Slowly going up and down until the back of her head ached from the pressure. The last thing Mike remembered was the loaded cum dripping from the bottom of Eve's mouth.

Chapter 14

Halley King is Mecklenburg's number one whore, she has mess with more niggaz than Super Head and Madonna put together. She came out of her crib wearing a black loose fitting blouse, tight blue jean shorts and no underwear. She knew that selling pussy was competitive and being a prostitute like herself has to be on top of her game. Halley also found this style of dress a dream fantasy for police sugar daddy's who rather trick than screw their old lady's. Halley strolled along Main Street Mecklenburg, hoping to catch a rich white man who likes black pussy before they thought about their long drive to the suburbs. She looked directly into the line of oncoming traffic, stood hip-shot and offered her best friendly pout. Four young white boys pulled up in a red and black mustang. She leaned into view them. She had been very paranoid of multiple customers since a group of MS-13 members from west

Charlotte, whooped her ass and raped her. "How much?" the kid in the driver's seat asked. "How many?" the boy in the passenger seat pulled down his jeans and waved his little white dick at Halley. "This many BITCCCHHH!" he screamed as the driver kicked the car into gear and took off. A box of empty beer cans flew out the window forcing Halley to duck. She heard them laughing all the way to the next light. Six years in the game had taught Halley a lot of things. The most important was to let shit ride. She thought about when she first met her pimp standing against his Cadillac, he had come into her life about the time her mother died. Not knowing any better she thought he wasn't shit. Not asking for any sex as they lay in the back seat of his car that first time. She wanted him to fuck her but he didn't, all he wanted was conversation. Over the years they became like friends. Not so well that he would change. Business was business, only one time did the relationship shook her. He was drunk and his wallet

slipped out of his front pocket, she noticed something

shiny and flicked it with her foot across the ground, it

was a badge. He explained that yeah he was a cop and

that pimping was his side hustle. "Besides," he said

with a smile. "We're not doing anything wrong are we? I

just help you sell pussy." they both glanced at each

other and laughed. As he guided her to his car, two

police cars drove past. Halley thought being close to a

cop might be worth it if this business ever got too hot

for her to handle.

Chapter 15

The street hustler whose mother threw him out

of the house at the age of fourteen has been in and out

of trouble ever since he was twelve years old, a drug

dealer and gang member. Redman was a suspect in a

number of armed robberies in the area. He took off his

shirt and tossed it in the grass beside the basketball court. "I got up next!" he shouted at some group of guys who were already on the court playing three on three. "We gotcha!" one shouted back from the court. Redman walked over to the other end of the court and waited for their game to end. "Is your name Redman?"

"Yeah why?"

"Detective Johnson Homicide, I need you to take a ride with me."

"Bullshit why the fuck do I need to ride with you for? I haven't done anything and besides, I'm trying to get some reck and you are jacking it off."

"I'm pretty sure you haven't Red but still I need you to come with me."

"Fuck that! If you don't have a warrant on me then you need to get the fuck out of my face," without responding Leroy reached over and grabbed Redman from behind his neck and dragged him to his car. "Now listen here nigga," gritting his teeth. "I'm not your average cop. I will beat your ass, take your dope and make you do a lifetime in prison for an ounce of coke without ever letting the DA see the dope or your black ass make it in the courtroom. You feel me now?"

"Yeah man."

"Now get the fuck in," with his hand still behind his neck he shoved Reds head first into the backseat of the car. "Where are we going?" asked Redman over the engine's roar. Water sprayed the windshield. "Nowhere in particular just need you to shut up and listen," said Leroy pulling out from the playground parking lot and down the road. "Now here is the deal, I'm going to need you to be my eyes and ears out..."

"Hold up for a second," Redman interrupted. I'm not a snitch."

"I'm not asking you to be a rat. Just shut the hell up and let me finish. We have a serial killer in Mecklenburg and I think he targets gang members and drug dealers like yourself, so what I need you to do is contact me if you see anything out of the ordinary." "Gotcha," replied Redman. Leroy pulled into a gas station and handed Redman his card. "Now get out."

"Hey man you not going to take me back?"

"You got dope money call a cab."

<u>Chapter 16</u>

Mike Surratt found himself in the center of the floor in a cold dark basement. The darkened room reeked of musty clothes and shoes. The sound of movement made the ceiling of the basement squeaked with each step. He started to move and immediately felt something hard around his ankle. "*What the fuck*," he thought. His hands cuffed behind his back with a long dog chain bind around his ankle attached to a heat pipe across the room. Lying on his back he managed to wiggle himself on his belly and wobble to one end of the floor. Mike tested the restraints carefully twisting his hand as far as he could. He thought about jerking his foot loose maybe breaking his ankle with one quick pull. "*Hell no too painful*," he thought. He yanked and pulled his hands but his effort only made the cuffs tighter and tighter tearing at his skin more and more. Blood dripped between the hand cuffs and he groaned. He couldn't even relax. All he could do was lean on the wall next to the pipes perfectly still staring ahead at the other end of the wall and chilled. He heard footsteps and voices, a man and a woman. "*That damn white bitch from the school*," he said to himself. Mike squinted when the bright light streamed in as the door opened. All he could see were two shadows. The figures walked towards him blocking off the light. Mikes eyes tried to readjust but couldn't do it fast enough to distinguish their features. In an instant they stood before him looking down. "What's up young buck?" the man said. "I am sorry kid but our boss wants you off the streets a sap," his sincere voice sent chills through Mike. He didn't sound violent but more like Chicken George off Roots. "But who is his boss and what does he want from me?"

"I wasn't acting in the car," the woman said. "I was really feeling you," the smell of weed smoke slightly breezed into Mike's nostrils. "You right this shit is some fire," she said. Taking a pull from the blunt and flicking it against a wall beside Mikes head. Mike was able to lower his eyes enough to see sweat soaking through her pants between her legs. Mike felt a strand of loose hair fall on his face. He looked up. "What the fuck do you want from me?" the two glanced at each other then back to Mike. "It's hard to explain kid," the man said. "It's not something that we or anyone else for that matter fully understands."

"You see Mike," Eve said calmly. "It's about keeping the hood safe from people like you."

"It's like Lewis said it's hard to explain." Mike's best friend Big Blue was shot and killed by a blood. Who waited in his apartment, he told Mike to chill with him that night at the club because he felt it was going to be some shit popping off. Since nothing happened he dropped Big Blue off at his apartment and that was the last time he saw Big Blue alive. Mike wondered if he would end up like his friend. Mike wondered if he will be laying behind a church pushing up daisies. He decided to keep them talking, something that he learned from watching The Heat of the Night. He used a confident voice. "Maybe I can pay you both double more than your boss if you just let me go."

"This nigga think were stupid Eve," said Lewis. "He thinks we're crazy, he thinks he can convince us to let him go. Next he's going to tell us that he has the whole town of Mecklenburg lock down." Lewis waited for Mike to speak. "I do have a stash behind my grandmother house. It looks that you both need the extra money, and no disrespect to you man but you need the money to buy you some new clothes cause that shit you got on looks like something off of Super fly." Lewis looked down at himself with embarrassment. "Ha' Ha' Ha 'we got jokes now huh?" Lewis said. "This is not Comic View young blood." Eve laughed and lightly touched Mike's left ass cheek. "Quit that you freak!" said Lewis. "Sorry LB I'm just horny." Mike couldn't figure these crazy people out. What are they?

Are they part of some gang? Folks, bloods, psychopaths, are they going to kill me? Mike began yanking his restraints uncontrollably. "Calm down young blood, just calm down," Lewis said. "Why? he looks so sexy doing that," said Eve. "I'm about to send your ass upstairs with Pam if you don't shut the hell up," said Lewis. "We're going to step out for a second Mike. So be on your best behavior," Lewis said. "Oh by the way, you can holler all you want no one will hear you, we're too deep in the country son."

"No wait!"

"Wait what?"

Don't leave, but we are the enemies why would you want us to stay that don't sound right do it?" said Eve.

"Well yeah, no... I mean..."

"Eve you're confusing the boy, just chill young buck we'll be back later."

"Well can you… uh can you get me some water to drink?"

"Well sure when we get back. Just swallow your spit for right now we wouldn't want you dying from dehydration now would we?"

Chapter 17

"Domino muthafucka it's my set!" shouted Lawrence looking up at the clock. "What the hell is taking Lewis so long to get here?"

"I don't know but my black ass is ready to eat," Divine said. Lawrence stood up from the table. "Y'all wait here for a second I'll be right back." he walked into the living room and picked up the phone to call Lewis. "Hey

Lawrence," a man called out from the kitchen table. "I quit I'm going out back and go see what's up with these hoes."

"Me too," another man said leaving Divine at the table by himself looking stupid. As both men headed out the back door, Divine got up from the table and walked in the living room where Lawrence was. "Is he at home?"

"Hell no, I don't have any idea where he could be." a flash of light zoomed across the front window and immediately catching Lawrence's attention. "Is that him?" Divine blurted out. "Yep that's him," said Lawrence peeping out between the window blinds. Lawrence immediately shot out the door and stood on the front porch. "Nigga what took you so long?" he said, arms spread out on both sides with a disappointed look on his face. Not responding Lewis glance his eyes at Lawrence flicking his hand at him as if he didn't care. "Can one of y'all help me with these bags?" Eve asked with both hands full struggling to shut the back car door. "Yeah sure," Pam jumped out from the passenger side and quickly walked over to the rear of the car and grabbed the last bag out the trunk. Placing his keys in his pocket and shutting the car door, Lewis waited while signaling the two ladies to hurry up. "We coming we coming just hold your horses," Pam said as she rushes to grab her purse out of the car. Lawrence just stood there with a shitty look on his face as the three approached the house. "Nigga you slow, it takes you an hour and a half to make a damn beer run," Lawrence said. "My bad dog I got tied up in something and lost track of time," Lewis replied. The door was wide open so Lewis was able to look in the house over Lawrence's shoulder. "Where's everybody at?"

"In the back waiting on you," Lawrence said as Lewis attempted to head inside. Lawrence immediately grabbed Lewis arm, pulling him close as if to whisper something in his ear. "Hey man which one of them you fucking?" cutting his eyes over at Pam's ass.

"The black chick."

"Damn!" turning his head away from Lewis. "You are one lucky muthafucka," he said as he steps aside viewing the two ladies as the three headed inside. Pam and Eve followed Lewis into the kitchen placing the bags on the table. The sound of Biggie Small's album Life after Death echoes through the whole house from out back. Pam grabbed the beers from out of the bags and put them in the fridge while Lewis snatched two from out of the fridge and handed one to Lawrence. As the four headed out the back door they could smell the aroma of barbecue chicken and hot dogs smoking on an open grill. "Hey Lewis!" a female shouted out. "Over here it's me Lisa." with a puzzled look on his face Lewis managed to spot Lisa underneath an oak tree standing beside two men. "Come here a minute there is someone I would like you to meet." Lisa called him LL because he resembled LL Cool J but at formal gatherings and in front of others she calls him by his real name. "What's up Lisa," Lewis gave her a hug. "How long has it been two, three years?"

"Something like that," replied Lisa. Pam eased up behind Lewis. "Who in the fuck is this bitch you talking too?" before Lewis could respond Lisa exploded. "Who in the hell is you calling a bitch? Bitch! I will beat your black ass out here," waving her hands uncontrollably. Pam reached around Lewis hitting Lisa in the mouth causing her to drop to her knees. Before she could get back to her feet Pam thrust her foot into Lisa's chest, she groaned and fell to the ground. Attempting to get on top of her Lewis immediately grabbed Pam's arm and pulled her away from the scene. "Woman what the hell is wrong with you? Do you have any idea who that was you just jumped on?"

"No."

"Well that was Detective Leroy Johnson's baby mama's sister. The same nigga that boss has plans for and I don't need you here fucking up shit. So what I need you to do right now is for you and Eve to go back to the house and handle that while I stay and clean up the mess you made." snatching her arm away, Pam gave Lewis a hateful look. "Okay nigga I gotcha but you didn't have to call me no bitch dough." as she walked away Lewis looked over at the crowd of people who were helping Lisa to her feet and thought. "*Damn Pam must know some shit*" because he's never seen a woman beat Lisa's ass and Lisa has beat a lot of bitches' asses in the past.

Chapter 18

Jason Martin had been picking up trash and scraping up dead animals off the main roads for

Spindale Correctional for the past four years and in them years he had found money, crack, weed and even one occasion he found a three-fifty seven in which he received fifteen merit days, a reward given to inmates who finds weapons or any illegal substances. So it came as no big surprise when he spotted something that resembled a manikin lying behind a guardrail underneath high grass and stick of briars. As he approached the limp figure its head down, arms out, legs splayed, he realized it wasn't a manikin at all but a young black boy. That wasn't new either, he has seen niggaz kidnapped, killed and thrown in ditches in the hood almost every day. He put down his bag of trash and poked the boy's leg with his foot. Jason didn't see the blood until the body flopped on its side or the knife sticking out his back. "C.O!" Jason shouted. "What boy?" the officer replied. "I think you need to come and see this." by the time Leroy arrived the Spindale Police were signaling traffic to go the other way. Spindale Police Sergeant Joseph Lincoln was in charge. Leroy met Joseph when they had worked a murder case together. After weeks of investigation Joseph finally cracked it by receiving an anonymous tip from the killer's mother. The man thought he could kill his wife and collect the life insurance that was worth over eighty five thousand dollars. "What's up Joseph?"

"How are you Detective?"

"What do you have?"

"He was found by prison road crew," Joseph said. "Killed somewhere else and dumped here, nasty job weird cuts on his chest. Belinda just left but your man Kelly still working," he said pointing to a figure hunched over the body. K.T. looked up and saw Leroy and signal him over and went back to work. Leroy who trusted Joseph filled him in on what's been going down.

"Leroy!" K.T. shouted. "Check this out." Both men walked to the body. "It's him," K.T. said. "Bible and everything, we got two indicators that might do us some good," KT said pointing to the boy's chest. "At first I thought they were knife cuts but there are ligature marks. It looks like he wove a wire over the boy's chest." Leroy turned the boy's head in his hands and his bloated tongue peeked out past dark blue lips. He presented a bloody spot on his cheek to the men. "I bet you it's from a finger." Leroy stood up with his head up in the air. "The nigga is now killing kids. That is something I don't like."

"Same here," KT said as he struggles to his feet. "I'll ride with him just to keep an eye on things." KT supervised the loading of the body into the medical examiners van, while Leroy paced back and forth. "Got a name?" Joseph found a school ID. "Mike Surratt, age seventeen, here is his address," Joseph ripped a page from his notebook and handed it to Leroy. "I'll send you our reports and photos this afternoon. I hope you get this clown. He is one sick dude," Joseph said. "I've got to wrap it up. I'll holler at you later."

"Alright take care." Joseph motioned his officers to leave the area while bystanders stood and watched the officers get in there vehicles and peel out.

.

Chapter 19

"What the hell are you talking about?" the voice on the phone said. "You said the Spindale House I was there," said Walker. No response. "Did you hear me?"

"Yes," the voice said. "But how many times have I've called you?"

"Hey isn't this—

"How many times, answer me bitch!" the voice on the phone shouted. "Twice," she replied nervously. "What's going on here I..."

"Mrs. Walker," the voice paused. "You have been played like a sucker which I'm afraid is going to cost the copycat dearly. We'll see which one of us is the real deal." Walker was confused. "You mean to tell me you didn't call me?" Walker asked. "No."

"Well how do I know it's you now?"

"Ask Detective Johnson about the Bible."

"The Bible, what is that supposed to mean?"

"Basic Instruction before leaving the earth, you must don't go to church?"

"No, I'm a Buddhist."

"That's understandable we do live in a diverse society."

"But you still haven't explained to me why you leave these Bible's at every crime scene?"

"They are tomb stones, it's like leaving my mark so to say."

"Can we meet somewhere? I can get your story on the news."

"Just chill we'll get to that another time Mrs. Walker. There's something that you need to be getting on top of."

"What's that?"

"The guardrail murder across from the old Wal-Mart in Spindale, expect an arrest, have your ass there when it happens."

"Did you.." the phone went dead.
"Hello…Hello…"

<u>Chapter 20</u>

A Spindale police office dropped off photos and reports taken at the guardrail murder. Leroy was about to call Dominos and order a hamburger pizza with extra cheese and olives when Belinda walked up on him. "Are those the reports and photos from Sergeant Joseph?" she asked. Leroy tossed the files on his desk and walked over to his chair. "Yup."

"Can I see the photos?"

"Help yourself," replied Leroy flopping into his chair observing as she scans through the photos. "What's up with this dude Leroy? Obviously he is not right in the head. What kind of serial killer do you know that goes around killing black gang members and drug dealers then leaving bibles on their bodies?"

"Crazy ass white folks that hates black people."

"That's not fair Leroy you don't know that for sure."

"Now Belinda look, the whole world knows that killer's in this fashion is a white man's occupation and that he's using this, I'm taking the law in my own hands bullshit to justify killing black people. So if you ask me I think we may have an Adolf Hitler on our hands."

"Hey, don't you dare make this into a black and white issue," Belinda said. "I'm not Belinda but you just can't think race is not an issue anymore just because our President is black," replied Leroy. "Maybe you're right." with a slight pause waving her finger at Leroy. "But you can't say that all serial killers are white people either, remember the D.C. sniper?"

"Oh yeah, but he was Jamaican."

"So what they still black," Belinda closed the folder. "Have you been by the boy's grandmother's house?"

"Not yet but that's my next move," said Leroy as he got up from his chair. "Are you still serious about snooping on that reporter?"

"Oh, been there done that, I got K.T. examining the recordings as we speak."

"I can't believe you just now telling me this."

"Sorry I thought K.T. told you."

"Well you just make sure you keep this between us, because if not we're dead."

"I gotcha." Belinda started to walk away. "Wait, I'm about to swing over to the boy's grandmother's crib and see what I can find out, want to ride?"

"I've got so much to do, but what the hell lets ride."

Mike Surratt lived with his grandmother in a run down one bedroom house across from a High School on Wells Avenue. The neighborhood looked quieted and peaceful during the day but at night niggaz rides through the neighborhood pushing dope and shooting crack heads for coming up short while others lock themselves inside away from the drug dealers and crack heads, whom floods the area. Leroy knocked on the door, an old fat light skin black woman holding a bowl of pig's feet open the door. "Hi I'm Detective Leroy Johnson, this is Lieutenant Bright," Leroy flashed his badge. The woman stopped eating and backed up into her house. "I can explain the whole thing. She told me I could use her food stamp card this month for watching her kids, so please don't cut my social security check off that's all I have," the old woman pleaded. "I will pay and…"

Leroy cut her off. "This isn't about a food stamp card m'am," he said. "Oh, thank you Jesus," with her hand on her chest. "Is Mike Surratt your grandson?"

"Yes, is he in some type of trouble?"

"No m'am do you mind if we come in?" Leroy asked. "Oh no come in." the woman took a few steps behind the door as the two walked in. "If he's not in trouble then what is this all about?" she said as she shut's the door behind them. "I'm sorry to tell you this m'am, but Mike was found murdered this morning." she dropped the bowl of pig's feet on the floor and slowly ran her shaking hand across her mouth staring at Leroy. "Oh Jesus! Why him lord? Why you take my baby?"

"Did Mike come home with anyone suspicious looking to you?" Leroy asked. "No, but are you sure it's him?"

"We found his school ID, we're sure." the old woman collapsed on the floor and began crying. "Mike! Oh Mike!" Belinda bent over to help the old woman off the floor. "Thank you sweetie," as she wiped tears off her face with her hand. "He was my only grandson."

"I know this is tough but you got to help us," Leroy said. "We wouldn't be doing this if it wasn't important." she rubbed her forehead. "Why? Why would someone kill my grandson? Was it over drugs? Please don't tell me he was on drugs. This neighborhood isn't so great but Mike always stayed at home at night." Leroy was tempted to lie and say Mike was mistaking for someone else and was accidently killed. He decided not to do that. "That's what we are trying to find out, did Mike come home last night?" she composed herself and spoke. "I'm not sure sometimes when he comes home at night I don't hear him because my medicine makes me sleep heavy, usually he be up in the morning playing his video games but sometimes he leaves early with his friends and I don't see him when I get up."

"Do you know where he went yesterday?"

"He said he was going to play basketball with a few friends of his."

"Do you know where?"

"I think…wait!" she thought for a second. "The Spindale House, that's it."

"May I use your phone?" Belinda asked. She pointed to the bedroom lamp table. "How did he get there?" Leroy asked. "Walked, Mike didn't own a car he didn't have money to buy a car he always begged me to buy him one but I just couldn't afford one." she began crying again. "Just a few more questions please." the old woman looked up. "Was Mike a trusting type of person, I mean would he jump into a car with someone he didn't know or get caught up in something he couldn't get out of?"

"If you asking me if he was street smart then yeah, he gave people the benefit of the doubt but he wasn't stupid he was always on point especially in this neighborhood. Did it happen around here?"

"We don't know his body was found behind a guardrail across from the old Wal-Mart."

"I use to take him to that Wal-Mart when he was a baby. That's where his mother and father met." Leroy shuddered. "You think there's a connection? I mean him being found near Wal-Mart," Belinda asked. "I don't think so, I believe that there is more to it," Leroy replied. "Oh God," the old woman began crying again. Leroy moved in to hold her. "Is there someone who can stay with you?"

"Yes my sister."

"Would you like me to call her for you?"

"No I'll do it." Belinda hung up the phone and walked out from the bedroom. She gave Leroy an okay with her fingers. "We're going now m'am we'll contact you just as soon as we catch this creep."

"I know y'all will," the old woman replied. Leroy and Belinda walked out the door. "I hate doing this Belinda."

"What's that?"

"Telling the victim's family that someone they love has been murdered."

"You right, it sucks. I think there's more to this than murdering gang members and drug dealers. You think the boy was a gang member?"

"I don't know but he is making a hell of a statement. This nigga keeps going and going and he doesn't stop. I think it's called lets fuck with Leroy head." a wave of tiredness swept over Leroy's face. "Did you get any information from the Spindale House?"

"The owner said he stopped by around six O' clock but didn't shoot any ball. He remembers him leaving thirty minutes later wearing a wife beater and shorts."

"It was warm that day he probably walked home," Leroy said. "I'll will chill at the area tonight and see if anyone saw him. I'll get K.T.'s lazy ass to come with me. Can you get somebody?" Belinda didn't answer as she opening up the car door. They both hopped in the car. "Well what's up can I get some help?"

"Yeah sure I can get at least one more for tonight, I'll will come too. I know a few folks in this area."

"Yeah right, who in the hell does your white ass know around here?" Leroy asked. Belinda hesitated. "If you want to know I dated a black guy from this area before." Leroy looked over at Belinda in surprised. "Was that before or after you seen jungle fever?"

<u>Chapter 21</u>

By twelve O' clock the media had sent reporters to the Spindale Police Department on Hill's Drive for a news conference. The murdered boy would certainly be the lead story for tomorrow's newspaper. Joseph stood in front of the police department. Microphones surrounded his face. "I'm Sergeant

Joseph Lincoln of the Spindale Police Department as most of you already know the body of a seventeen year old boy, a Spindale resident was found dead by a prison inmate while working on the road crew this morning at approximately eight O' clock on highway 119 across from the old Wal-Mart. We are withholding his identity until we notify the victim's family. I'll be glad to take your questions."

"Sergeant!" a reporter shouted. "Was the killing gang or drug related?"

"We believe that it may be gang related because according to our resources he was believed to be affiliated with the Crips, a dangerous street gang who are well known in the area."

"Can you tell us how he was murdered?" Joseph didn't want to be graphic but he had no choice. "We believe the killing took place somewhere else, where the victim was stabbed multiple times in the back with a twelve inch knife and tossed behind a guardrail on highway 119, but again we want know the cause of death until the medical examiner completes his report."

"Preliminary findings also show evidence of a possible suffocation."

"Let me emphasize," Joseph raised his voice. "That these are preliminary findings." after fifteen minutes the crowd became restless. Noticing this Joseph said. "If there isn't anything further…"

"One last question," Tina walker cleared her throat. "Tina Walker Eyewitness News, I understand that this murder is connected to two other homicides of young black men that recently occurred in the district am I right?"

"I have no knowledge of other homicides in the district you will have to talk to the Mecklenburg Police."

"Why aren't they here Sergeant?" Walker said. "This is their case isn't it?" the crowd stirred and turned their attention to Walker and Joseph. "Spindale Police asked me to conduct this press conference because the body was found in our jurisdiction and we conducted the preliminary investigation. We have since turned our case over to Mecklenburg Homicide as required by law," Joseph looked around. "Now if there are no further questions."

"I have another question," Walker said. "Can you tell us if anything unusual was found at the scene?" she couldn't mention the bible without revealing her source to other reporters. She was going to keep that to herself. Joseph knew about the bible but he didn't show any acknowledgement. "I'm not sure I understand what you are asking."

"Well the question is plain as day," Walker said in a condescending tone. "Was anything strange found?" the crowd of reporter's stirred tense. "Mrs.

Walker," Joseph began. "I would call a brutally

murdered black boy found behind a guardrail rather

strange wouldn't you?" the crowd laughed as Joseph

excused himself and headed up the steps toward the

department entrance. Walker ran and stopped him.

"You know what the hell I'm talking about the bible,"

she said. Joseph looked her in the face and giggled.

"I'm sorry but I don't believe in the bible. I'm atheist; I

have some where to go excuse me." Joseph was out of

ear range in an instant but Walker cursed him anyway.

"Fuck you!" a reporter from the Charlotte station tapped

her on the arm. "Good going Connie Chung." Walker

ignored the sarcasm and called to her crew. "Why in

the hell are y'all just standing there for?" Walker said.

"Get y'all shit and meet me at the police headquarters

in Mecklenburg and don't stop for nothing on the way."

they watched her get in her car and peel out. Walker

arrived at the police headquarters and went straight to Cox's office. "My staff was just over at Spindale Police Headquarters for a news conference and that lame ass Sergeant Joseph tried to play me." Tina Walker sat in a wooden chair in Cox's office. "What do you want me to do Mrs. Walker?" Cox asked. "Well for one you and Detective Johnson need to stop trying to make me look like a fool. I know about the bible left at the murder scenes, B-I-B-L-E break it down. Basic, instructions, before, leaving, earth. He wants you and your men to follow some type of instruction before he kills. It's like some type of game he's playing." Cox applied a poker face. "And I know that he has some type of beef with Detective Johnson. I'm the only person outside the police and the killer of course who can prove it."

"So what are you trying to say?" Cox said sharply. "What I am saying is, I can go with the killer and the Johnson connection story and the public will eat it up. But for the right price I will keep the story on the low."

"And what would that price be?" Cox asked. "That depends if your men are smart enough to catch this creep."

"Oh we will," Cox replied. "Okay, if you are so sure of yourself Mr. Action Jackson. I want to be there when he's caught. I mean an exclusive coverage of the killer's arrest. Advanced notice, cameras the whole nine yards that's the deal."

"Assuming that we make an arrest, and we will. Why should I make this deal? Why should I care if you tell the whole state of North Carolina?" Walker leaned forward in her chair looking Cox in the eye. "Because it wouldn't look good for your department knowing that there is a serial killer in Mecklenburg who may be friends with your head Detective Leroy Johnson,"

Walker said. "C'mon that's ridiculous lady. You know that's not true," Cox said with a hilarious look on his face. "Are you sure about that Captain, are you sure if a story like this reached your superior that he wouldn't ask questions about Detective Johnson loyalty to the department. Can you picture the deadlines going across your TV set," using her hands to demonstrate. "Detective Johnson, ex-prisoner connected to a... Cox interrupted. "Alright, alright you made your point. It seems that you would hurt anybody for a story Mrs. Walker."

"It's a dirty game Captain, but somebody has to do it."

"You bitch."

"I'll be that," Walker smiled. "Here's my card," she said dropping it on his desk as she stood up. "You know what it is, keep in touch." as she closed the door

Cox shouted into his phone. "Find Johnson for me right now!" Leroy and Belinda were driving back from Mike Surratt's grandmother's house when Leroy's cell phone rang. The phone number for communications flashed across his caller ID, Leroy answer. "Hello this is Detective Leroy John…"

"Where are you?" Cox asked. "On highway 74 heading home, what do you need?"

"I need to talk to you, check in immediately with me when you get a chance," Cox said. Leroy turned to Belinda. "That nigga sounds funny on the phone. He didn't sound like Cox. He sounded almost normal he wants to see me."

"For real what do you think he wants?"

"I will find out in just a minute." Leroy pulled his car into a diagonal space marked for police vehicles only. They walked into the building, Leroy seen Walker outside the door smoking a cigarette but didn't say anything. The two had never met face to face and Leroy preferred it that way. For the first time ever Leroy sensed fear in Cox's face. Gone was the unbreakable Negro. "I had no choice," said Cox after he described his meeting with Walker. "If she goes on tonight with the connection with you, the killer, and the bible mess our case and our ass is done."

"How in the hell does she know so much?" Belinda asked. "I don't know probably the killer told her who else?"

"Yeah right," said Leroy. "Chill out Leroy I'm not in the mood," Cox said. "I can tell you that I'm not happy about Walker coming into my office giving me ultimatums that is unethical."

"What do you think we need to do?" Belinda asked. "What we need to do is catch the muthafucka."

"I agree," said Leroy reaching for the phone on Cox's desk. "You don't mind if I use your phone?"

"No, but do you mind if I ask who you are calling?"

"I'm calling KT about the finger print."

"Finger print, what finger---?" Leroy interrupted him by placing his finger to his lips signaling Cox to shut up. "Okay thank you very much bye."

"What did he say?" Belinda asked. "That was the lab assistant she said that he is on his way here."

Fifteen minutes later KT knocked on the door and entered without being invited. He looked around and saw everyone just sitting there looking stupid. "My bad I must be in the wrong room. I thought this was Captain Cox's office." nobody responded.

Finally Cox spoke "Boy get your mulatto ass in here and tell me what you got."

"The reports came in, I have a positive match and ID." he handed Cox an index card which the Captain looked over and then passed it to Belinda. She studied it and handed it to Leroy. "Are you sure it's right?" Belinda asked. "I'm sure."

"This shit doesn't add up," Leroy said. "What do you mean it don't add up?" KT asked. "What I mean is that this man is to damn smart to leave a print around for us to find."

"You are the one who found it."

"I know I'm just saying."

"Anybody can slip up," Cox said. "What do we have on the suspect?" KT handed him a file folder. Cox flipped through the pages. "Four priors for assault and battery, probation on the first two then he did three years in South Carolina been straight ever since, last known address was Highland Parks."

"We can get a search warrant in no time," Belinda said. "Fuck the warrant lets go down there and check it out," Leroy said. "I hate to say Leroy is right, we don't have time for that let's just go," KT said. "We can't do that if it gets out that we searched a man's house without a warrant we'll all going to be drawing unemployment checks, It's already bad enough that Walker has us in her back' pocket," said Belinda

"Man damn that bitch!" Leroy exploded. "Let's just do our thang and let Walker do her thang, if she wants to talk let her talk because I don't give a damn."

"Leroy you wrong on this one considering your past and her story, it's not going to look good. It's a chance y'all can be suspend," Cox said. "So what, it's not like I'm behind on my rent. Let's just do this and get it over with. If you call that woman then you're dumb," Leroy looked over at Belinda and KT. "What the hell is y'all standing there looking stupid for, come on." he left and slammed the door so hard the wall shook. "I'm sorry Captain," said KT heading out the door behind Leroy. "Belinda go with him I want this ass hole and I want him now," Cox said. Belinda left behind KT.

His office now quiet Cox picked up the phone, then immediately put it down. "Shit," he sat for a minute staring at a picture of him and his wife and kids thinking. "Fuck it," he picked up the phone and dialed. "May I speak with Tina Walker please?"

<u>**Chapter 22**</u>

Without a search warrant Leroy and Belinda drove to the residence in Highland Park. Belinda radioed for a canine unit. "Why in the hell did you call for a canine unit? We are looking for a killer not drugs," Leroy said. "I'm just going by the procedures."

"Is not having a search warrant going by procedure," Leroy asked. Belinda ignored the sarcastic remark and they both jumped out the car, pointing at the back of the house. Leroy began signaling Belinda to check the back. Leroy thought if only he was alone he could catch the killer, beat him down, make him confess to the murders and confiscate anything of value that he could put back on the streets for profit. Guns drugs you name it. Just because he's a police officer didn't mean he was a saint. He was still one hundred percent hood. About a minute later a woman's voice spoke through Leroy's CB radio. "The back yard is cleared." Leroy responded. "Gotcha we're going in."

Belinda came around the front to join Leroy, pistol

drawn. Both walking softly on the porch of the brick

frame house, Leroy knocked and announced himself.

No answer. He peered through the widow and was

startled by a spider crawling across the window frame.

Leroy holstered this weapon. "Stand back Belinda." as

he positions himself. Leroy took his twelve and a half

size foot and kicked the door open. Once inside Belinda

held her pistol up against her chest and walked briskly

to the back door, unlocked it and let the officer who just

arrived in. Leroy motioned the one with the dog to

search the house. The German shepherd strained his

leash sniffing around doors and cloths that were on the

floor and poking behind the sofa. Belinda searched for

a basement door and found one. Belinda ordered the

dog handler to go down and take a look, the dog and

his handler scurried down the stairs into the basement.

They returned several minutes later, the officer announced that the basement is clear but added. "You better take a look down there." Leroy and Belinda walked down into the basement. It stunk like shit from old unwashed clothes laying in the floor. At the far end of the basement were several bibles torn in half. Black and white photos of black males hand cuffed with their brains blown out dangle from a string which was attached to the ceiling fan. Belinda opened a red tool box that sat next to an abandoned washing machine and found newspaper clipping of some of Leroy career achievements as a police officer and other clippings of the three murders. Someone had underlined the descriptions of the weapons that were used and the injuries that were made. "Leroy take a look at…."

"Say cheese." Leroy and Belinda spun around. "Damn KT quit playing," said Belinda. "Showtime," KT said jokingly holding up his camera. He quickly lost his smile as he looked around. "What the hell." Belinda and Leroy headed upstairs to let KT take his shots. "Cox was right, smart people do slip Leroy," said Belinda. A voice on Leroy's CB called. "A truck is coming in the driveway."

"Get him," Leroy said as he and Belinda ran upstairs out of the basement. "Hey what the hell is going on here?" the man shouted as he reached the damaged door. Leroy and Belinda confronted him "Is this your crib?" Leroy asked. "Yeah, who are you?"

"As if you don't know I'm Detective Johnson, we are here to search your house."

"What the hell for? I would like to see a warrant if you don't mind," Lewis said. He tossed a six pack of beer on the couch. He was dressed in sweat pants, shirt and flip flops. "Where were you last night Mr. Brooks?"

"None of your damn business Uncle Tom you still haven't shown me a search warrant."

"Just give us a minute we gotcha," replied Leroy. Just then KT came out of the basement carrying his camera and a plastic trash bag.

"Done," he said to Leroy. "You done with what man, what the fuck were you doing down there?" he started for the basement door but Leroy stopped him by putting his hand on his shoulder. "Just fall back homeboy."

"Y'all just can't come in a niggaz house without a warrant and just…."

"Just chill homeboy. Why don't you tell us what you do for a living?"

"Work, that's what the fuck I do for a living."

"You call stalking me, and tearing up bibles work?"

"Man kiss my ass you can't…"

Suddenly Leroy pushed Lewis up against the wall. "I do what the hell I want to do because I'm the police nigga," Leroy said. Lewis lowered his head. "I like reading different bibles and keeping up with your career. You can say I'm a fan."

"You trying to be funny boy?" as he pushes him up against the wall again. "No man I'm just saying there is no law against it."

"But there is a law against killing niggaz," said Leroy. "Man I don't know what the hell you are talking about."

"We'll see," said Leroy. "Why don't we start with where you were last night?"

"I told you man none of your damn business."

"We can talk now or go down town it's your choice," Leroy said. "I'm not saying shit." Leroy motioned for his officer to handcuff Lewis and take him away. "Read him his rights."

"I'm going to sue the shit out of you Detective," shouted Lewis as he was led away. "You got the wrong man!" he shouted again. Standing together in the house Leroy turned to Belinda. "The guy may be telling the truth." Belinda started to say something when they heard Lewis big mouth yelling outside.

Walker and her staff were filming the officers putting Lewis into the car. Walker said to the camera. "You've just seen it, Lewis Brooks taking away in the connection with the killing of three people in the Mecklenburg area. He's been called the Bible Killer by police because he leaves bibles at the scene of the crime. Why he does that is still a mystery." Walker turned away from the camera. "Coming out of his house is head Detective Leroy Johnson the man of the hour," Walker ran to him. "Detective," she said breathlessly. "We understand that Lewis Brooks is the prime suspect in the three murders. What led you to him?" Leroy kept walking in a fast pace. Walker had trouble keeping up, camera man right behind the two. "Brooks has had a past record of assaults, can you enlighten us on that?" Leroy gave her the finger and slammed his car door almost catching Walkers hand. Belinda jumped into the passenger side. "As you can see the police are keeping quiet about this interesting case. We will have an update on the seven O' clock news report. This is Tina Walker reporting for Eyewitness News."

"Annnd clear!" said Jabril. "That work well," Walker said. "Now let's get down to the police station for some more information." the two technicians grabbed their gear. "What do you think about this bible mess?" Jabril said to his partner. "Some crazy shit if you ask me." J.J said. "Maybe he wants to send them to heaven before he kills them."

"You wrong for that Jabril," said J.J.

Chapter 23

Leroy and Belinda drove back to the police station listening to Tupac while Leroy rhythmically chanted the lyrics. Finally turning down the music, Leroy broke out with a small giggle. "You know what Belinda?" as he glanced over at her. "What's that?" replied Belinda. "Nothing really, it's just that he's not our man. I don't know how he did it, but he played us."

"What do you mean he played us?"

"The real killer who else, this Lewis guy is just somebody to throw us off track."

"You really believe that?" Belinda said. "You damn right, I'm not saying that this guy is not involved, it's just that he's not the head nigga in charge," Leroy said. "You might be right Leroy but I don't know," Belinda said shaking her head back and forth.

As they approached the building they saw reporters getting out of their vehicles setting up there equipment. "It seems that they don't waste anytime do they?" Leroy said. "Let's go around back," Belinda said. Leroy pulled around the police station and they took the stairs to the second floor, a circus of reporters was waiting in front of the station talking to the officers who were coming in and out of the department. Speaking to one office that had a little bit of insight on the case was Sergeant Jacob Hayes. "Captain Cox will make a statement in about ten minutes," his voice barley heard above the crowd. "All I can tell you now is that we have a suspect and he is being questioned." inside Lewis Brooks was placed in a holding cell while Captain Cox and another officer were talking. They saw Leroy and Belinda who walked in through an exit back door. Cox then immediately order the officer to remove the suspect out of the holding cell and into the interrogation room. "Hold on for a minute I will be right back," Leroy said to Belinda. Leroy stepped over into Cox's office. "Man why in the hell did you call that reporter, it looks like a damn concert going on outside."

"So what, we got him didn't we? From what the officer tells me it's a done deal for this guy."

"Done deal my ass, it's not him."

"Do you have any proof it's not him?"

"Well no."

"Okay, don't make yourself look like a fool with your theories. You should be happy with yourself," said Cox as he walked away out of his officer. Leroy ignored what Cox said and dialed the desk officer. "This is Johnson would you send the Lewis' prints to KT thanks." Leroy took a deep breath and headed into the interrogation room. Lewis sat in front of a small table nervously eating away at his finger nails slouched in his chair. As Leroy studied his face, it became clear to him that Lewis was either a sociopathic liar who felt he could con his way around an interrogation or has actually convinced himself that he was innocent and had nothing to worry about from answering questions. "Where were you last night Mr. Lewis around nine O' clock?" Leroy asked. Lewis looked at Leroy and he flexed his right arm muscle which had a tattoo of a cross. "I was at a cookout with some old friends of mine."

"How about you tell me the names of these friends of yours?" Lewis lowered his head down squeezing his mouth tightly shut as if he was about to cuss Leroy out. "Man I don't know their real names. I just know what they go by on the streets."

"Then what do they go by on the streets?" Leroy asked. Lewis started to respond until KT knocked and came in, he whispered to Leroy. "Brook's prints taken downstairs matched the finger print on Mike's cheek." KT handed Leroy the print cards and left. Without saying anything else Leroy glanced at the cards and looked over at Lewis. "Okay homeboy give me some names." Lewis leaned back in his chair arms folded. "It's Dirty, True self, and Supreme." Leroy unplugged the surveillance camera and walked over on the other side of the table where Lewis was and smile in his face. "Now you wouldn't be lying to me would you?" shaking his head Lewis looked up at Leroy, "Nah man that is the truth."

"So it's the truth that you don't know anything about a young boy being killed and tossed behind a guardrail either do you?"

"Nope!" said Lewis arrogantly. Without saying another word Leroy immediately snatched Lewis out of his chair slamming him to the floor, finger print cards laying everywhere, with both hands tightly around Lewis' neck. Leroy looked back at the door to make sure no one heard the loud tumble. "Now you listen here nigga, a young boy was found dead this morning and on his cheek was your finger print in blood." he grabbed one of the scattered cards off the floor. "Look here you muthafucka," sticking the card real close to Lewis' face. "Your prints match the print found on the boy's cheek how do you explain that?" Lewis' eyes widened his hands shook. "That's my word on everything I love I didn't do it. I was at a cookout."

"If not you then who was it?"

"Ah…Ah…"

"Tell me dammit or I will break your legs!" Leroy said. Before Lewis could respond Cox walked through the door. "Get the hell off of him Detective!" shouted Cox. "Have you lost your mind?"

"I'm sorry Captain but I…"

"Just shut up!" Cox interrupted. "I want this interrogation terminated immediately Detective." while Leroy kept his eyes on Lewis, Cox stepped outside and motioned for an officer. "Take him to holding." Cox looked over at Leroy pointing his finger at him. "You in my office now!" shouted Cox. As the two walked between a row of desks past detectives who were working the phones and giving interviews, finally in his office. Cox ordered Leroy to have a seat. "Now what was that all about?"

"It was nothing I just lost my temper a little bit. It won't happen again."

"It better not because we can't afford a lawsuit, besides what did you get out of him?"

"Well not much but I think if I…" suddenly they were interrupted by a knock on the door. "Come in!" shouted Cox. "Sorry to interrupt you two, but our suspect said he knows how his fingerprint got on the boys cheek," said Belinda with just her head stuck inside Cox's office. "For real," said Leroy. "Yeah, but what's funny is he only wants to talk to you."

Chapter 24

"Will you hurry the hell up woman it's getting late and we don't have that much time."

"I'm coming, I'm coming just give me a minute to get organized," Eve replied as she skims through her leather attaché case. "I know it is here somewhere."

"What are you looking for?" the man asked. Eve ignored the man's question and took out a pink document which read in fine dark print on the front, <u>DORTHEA DIX INSTITUTION.</u> Looking over the document to make sure that everything was right and exact. She held the form up. "Here you go you're going to need this." the man walked over to Eve and grabbed the pink form without taking time to look at it. He immediately placed the pink paper in his back pocket, and the two headed inside the police station. Once inside the man quietly said to Eve. "Remember to try to keep a straight face and act professional cause any little thing can give us away." Eve looked over at the man nodding her head in acknowledgment. Approaching the front desk Eve immediately introduce herself. "Hi, my name is Dana Foster Attorney of law. I represent Lewis Brooks, I understand that y'all have my client here in custody," Eve gave the desk officer her card to support her claim. The officer glanced at the card and handed it back to Eve. "Just one moment please," the desk lady said just before she started to speak into the intercom. She paused and turn her attention to the gentleman who was standing next to Eve. "And may I ask who you are?"

"Oh yes, I'm sorry my name is Dr. James Spear, Mr. Brooks is a patient of mine at the Cleveland County Medical Center here is my....."

"That's okay," she interrupted as she flicked her hand to suggest he keep whatever he had to show her. As she lowered her face into the loud speaker she called for the arresting officer. "Detective Johnson report to booking, Detective Johnson report to booking." the sound of the announcement echoed through the whole facility. "Just have a seat in the lobby Detective Johnson should be down here any minute now," she said. As the two headed into the lobby Eve turned to the man to express her concern. "Do you not think using that name is playing it a little bit too close?" she whispered. "Don't worry I have everything under control," replied the man. After waiting about ten minutes Leroy finally made it down to booking to speak to the desk officer. Before Leroy could say a word he was immediately told that two people were waiting on him in the lobby. As he headed towards that direction the two quickly spotted Detective Johnson and decided to meet him halfway. "Hello Detective my name is Dana Foster. I'm an attorney from Kings Mountain and with me is Dr. James Spears of the Cleveland County Medical Center. I guess you already know we are here on the behalf of Lewis Brooks. I understand that my client was arrested today in the connection of three homicides in which I can prove to you right now that Mr. Brooks has been in a mental institution for the past eight months and was just released this morning." clearing his throat Leroy finally spoke. "Well lady technically Mr. Brooks hasn't been charged with anything other than being a person of interest."

"Well Detective I surely have something here to prove that you have the wrong man." Eve reached into her attaché case and grabbed three signified documents and handed them to Leroy. After a couple of minutes of studying the forms he handed them back to Eve and turned his attention to the man. "Let me guess you must be his shrink?" Leroy said. "I wouldn't say shrink," the man giggled. "That word sounds a little insulting. I would prefer to say that I am his friend Detective." feeling that the man's voice sound familiar. "Have we meet somewhere before Doc?" Leroy asked. "No, I don't believe we have unless you are an old patient of mine," the man said jokingly. But Leroy wasn't laughing. "If you smart you'll watch your mouth," Leroy said hatefully. "Now do you have anything to support what this lady has said?"

"Of course I do." the man immediately reached into his back pocket and handed Leroy a pink document. "I have been Mr. Brook's psychiatrist for the past fifteen years," the man added. As Leroy handed him back the pink paper. Leroy took his hand and rubbed it across his face to express he was tired and exhausted and that all he wanted to do now is go home and go to sleep. Glancing at his watch Leroy motioned for the two to follow him to the second floor to speak with the Captain.

In his office Cox was on the phone with his wife. "Yes baby something came up and it seems that I will not be home until late. Okay love you too bye." Cox hung up the phone and was about to make another call but it was interrupted by a knock at the door. "Come in," said Cox. Stepping into his office, Leroy immediately shut the door behind him while the two waited outside Cox's office. "We have a problem Captain."

"What type of problem?" Cox asked. "It seems that Mr. Brooks may have a possible alibi."

"What other possible alibi could he have Detective?"

"It seems that according to these forms the guy was in Dorothea Dix for the last eight months and was just released at six O' clock this morning," Leroy said.

"Dammit! Who gave you this shit? Cox asked. "His lawyer and Dr. Phil, they are right now waiting outside your office. "Fuck!" said Cox as he slammed his fist on the desk. "You mean to tell me that we have a coconut in custody instead of a killer?"

"Not exactly because it doesn't explain why Brooks fingerprint was on the victim's cheek."

"Maybe KT made a mistake," Cox said. "I doubt that," said Leroy. "The prints were double checked."

"So if there's no mistake then that would mean that the forms I have here are fake and the assholes outside my office are cons."

"Yup, at first the two had me fooled with their gift of gab until I notice that the good O" Dr. James Spears is out there wearing a disguise."

"What makes you think that?" Cox asked. "What nigga you know goes around wearing a twelve inch white beard with long white hair and funny colored eyes? The damn nigga looks like a black Uncle Sam." Cox wanted to laugh but kept his composure. "What I think is that the real killer doesn't believe that Brooks can keep his mouth shut long enough to let shit blow over so he sent these two clowns to help him con his way out of here." Cox thought for a few seconds and stood up from his chair. "Well that's not going to happen." Cox started to walk from behind his desk. "Wait, what are you about to do?"

"What do you think, I'm going out here an end this charade of theirs."

"Just chill, I got a better idea."

"And what's that?" Cox replied. "Let the suspect go."

"Ah hell no. let's just go out there and lock their asses up," Cox said angrily. "That wouldn't be a good idea because the killer would still be out there. The only thing we would have is these three clowns. So let's just play their game for right now and see what happens."

"You mean let them play us like suckers?"

"Well the only way to catch a sucker is to play like one," said Leroy. Cox sat back in his chair and propped his feet on the desk. "Alright Detective I'll go along with this plan of yours and I'll run this across Belinda and KT. But I warn you…" as he pointed his finger at Leroy. "If you haven't caught this guy in the next three or four days, I'm taking you off…" but before he could finish his sentence the phone rang and Cox immediately took the call. Suggesting that the call was important Leroy immediately waved his hand up at Cox and left his office.

Chapter 25

While waiting patiently in a holding cell Lewis couldn't ignore the graffiti all over the wall with its gang related expression and violent content. While glancing at the symbols he thought about what he could say or do to get himself out of this tight situation, even if it means giving up his sixty-five year old mother who has been selling dope for twenty five years on Amazon road in Mecklenburg but whatever it may be he was not going back to prison. Lewis stood up from the bench and walked over to the cell door where there was an intercom up in the right hand corner, leaning his mouth into the intercom he requested to see Detective Johnson. "Just one moment please," the sound of a female voice responded back. Several minutes later two officers came through the door. "Mr. Brooks," said one of the officers. "This must be your lucky day your free to go." thirty minutes later Brooks was down in booking receiving his belongings and was heading out the door and into a white Lincoln. As they pulled off, there was total silence. Finally Lewis spoke "Boss I want to let you know I didn't say shit. That's my word." no response. Lewis reached into his pocket and took out a cigarette. "Let me get a light someone." Eve fumbled around in her purse and grabbed a silver and gold lighter and handed it to Lewis. "I appreciate," said Lewis rolling down the window. Lewis lit his cigarette and handed the lighter back to Eve. "Alright, what did I do?"

"It's what you didn't do," Eve replied. "And what's that?"

"You weren't careful," said the man in the passenger seat jumping into the conversation. "You let them catch you and that's not good for the home team."

"I can explain boss. I... I..."

"Shut the fuck up!" the man said. "We just con Detective Johnson into letting you go and knowing Leroy it won't be long until he realized that."

"What do you suggest we do?" Lewis asked. After a few seconds of silence the man spoke. "I may have to get rid of you." Lewis immediately tried to jump out of the car but the door was jammed. "It's no use nigga it's locked from the outside."

"Please boss don't do this give me one more chance." the man turned to Lewis with a pistol in his face. "I'm sorry Lewis it had to come to this." Lewis could only close his eyes.

Chapter 26

Leroy sat in the living room reading the morning newspaper. He was still sleepy but not so out of it that he couldn't make out the Mecklenburg Post headline: *Bible Killer Suspect Released*. He wiped the cold from his eyes and read the story.

In a highly unusual action district police yesterday arrested then quickly released their prime suspect in three brutal slayings of black men in the Mecklenburg circle area. Officials said that Lewis Brooks, 38 was a strong suspect in the so-called "Bible Killer" murders until police discovered that the suspect had a concrete alibi, according to homicide Captain David Cox, Brooks who has been convicted of previous assaults on people. Was arrested based on finger prints found yesterday at the scene. The body of Mike Surratt, 17 was discovered on HWY 119 behind a guardrail across from the old Wal-Mart by a prison worker at Spindale Correctional. Cox declined to elaborate on the nature of the alibi but said "The situation was out of their hands." police have described the murderer as the "Bible Killer" because he leaves bibles at the murder scenes. We don't know why

he does it.

The article jumped to pages three and four and included pictures of the four victims and a map of where their bodies were found. April interrupted his reading. "Want some coffee?" she asked coming down the stairs into the living room and into the kitchen. "Yeah straight black no cream." April poured the coffee and went back into the living room and sat down next to Leroy. "Here you go," she said handing him the cup of coffee and grabbing the paper out of his lap. "Leroy is you sure you know what you are doing?" she paused for a minute and then added. "I mean why in the hell y'all let this crazy nigga go? It's obvious he is guilty as shit."

"He's guilty by affiliation, but not murder."

"What makes you say that?"

"Because who every the killer is knows me personally."

"That's bullshit Leroy."

"Then how can you explain why my name keeps coming up in his letters?"

"Maybe he only wants you to catch him."

"Then why doesn't he just send me a letter telling me where to meet him so I can shoot his ass?" Leroy said. "I guess he wants to make you look stupid first by sending you those letters and leaving bibles around like clues," April said. "Clues, what do you mean clues?"

"You know the ones that the riddle uses to send Batman."

"C'mon April this is real life shit, not fantasy but I understand what you're saying, but then again you maybe on to something." Leroy stood up and kissed April on the cheek. "You are a genius."

"What, I don't understand?" April said curiously. "I have to get ready for work and I won't be back till late." Leroy finished his coffee and headed up stairs without saying another word.

Chapter 27

Leroy's answer machine on his desk was filled with messages from almost every reporter in the state of North Carolina. His first thought was to delete them but instead, said fuck it and kept his focus on the issue at hand. He thought about what April had said about the letters being clues. He got his text books and work sheets that he used in profiling school along with an old black bible that he kept on top of his filing cabinet. Leroy hadn't worked a profile since profiling school and that's because he felt it was too much work. He started to reread his notes but for an instance his concentration was knocked off point by one of the killers riddle like letters. "*To know my first name, take it back to 1611, my first name ordered me to write my last name and age in it*" Intuitively Leroy thought he knew what the profiling would tell him. But going through the exercise would make certain. He also looked at it as a chance to go over the letters and maybe see something that he hadn't seen before. In his mind he knew that there was a connection between the bible and the letters. Isn't that what April had said. He wasn't going to be happy until he found that connection. Leroy readjusted the light from a gooseneck lamp on the desk and sorted his papers. The notes were sloppy and he had trouble reading them. He turned his attention to one letter that was written in red ink. What puzzled him was the second sentence. "*Follow the basic instruction before you leave this earth nigga because it's been the law since 1611"*

"It doesn't make since" he thought to himself. What does 1611 have to do with the death of three innocent people? "This shit is crazy." he muttered to himself. Suddenly his cell phone rang. "Dammit, who in the---" glancing at his caller ID it was his mom dukes, deciding if he should take the call or not. He immediately realized that his mother was a woman who could pretty much solve anything giving the fact that she's been on a number of game shows and even won a round on jeopardy. If anyone could help him it would be her. He pushed the send button and put the phone on the loudspeaker. "What's up mom?"

"Oh hi baby I was just calling to see how you was doing."

"Yeah right mom you never call to see how I'm doing so what's your problem?" Leroy said coldly. "Ah, well wait a minute. Son is your phone on loudspeaker because I can hear people in the back ground?"

"Mom," he interrupted. "Okay, okay well the reason I called is that I need some money to pay off some bills."

"Money, how much money are you talking about?" she hesitated for a second and then spoke. "About a few hundred dollars just till next week."

"A few hundred dollars," Leroy said raising his voice a little. "I mean I'll pay you back next week I promise." there was a silence between the two for a second. Finally Leroy spoke. "Alright I will see what I can do."

"Oh baby thank you I will make sure you have your money back and some trust me," she paused then added. "Well I got to go I will talk to you later bye." she was about to hang up until Leroy blurted out. "Oh before you go. I need you to help me with something."

"And what's that?"

"Well it's a little complicated."

"Boy, just tell me what's on your mind."

"Well it's about a case I'm working on and…"

"Oh I bet it's about that bible killer isn't it?" she said excitedly. "Yeah mom, I been…"

"Why does he leave bibles around for?"

"I don't know mom, that's what I'm trying to figure out if you would just let me finish."

"Oh, I'm sorry for cutting you off. Go ahead son," she added. "As I was saying I have been racking my brain trying to figure out the meaning of these letters."

"What letters?"

"The ones that were written by…"

he pauses. "Well you know."

"Oh I see, well what do they say?" Leroy search around over his desk for a letter. "Here we go this one says, "*to know my first name take it back to 1611, my first name ordered me to write my last name and age in it*" now I think that this letter I just read has something to do with the bible."

"Hmm," she pause as if to give herself a few seconds to think. "You right because 1611 is the year when the King James Bible was authorized."

"You mean to tell me that the bible was written by King James and he is trying to tell me he's the incarnation of the late King James of England?"

"No boy, what this guy is saying is that James is his first name and to figure out his last name you must figure out who King James ordered to write the bible."

"Man this guy is clever." not wanting to use the N-word in front of his mother. "So you don't know who King James ordered to write the bible?"

"No but I got a hunch, give me a couple of days to do some research to know for certain."

"Well give me your hunch."

"No I'm not going to do that because I may be wrong and I don't want you locking up the wrong guy."

"Well I understand, just let me know something as soon as possible."

"Oh I will son."

"Well okay I will talk to you later bye." Leroy pushed the end button on his cell phone and placed it back into his pocket, leaning back in his chair he thought who could this nigga be? *I need to think, could this nigga really be somebody I know, no way in hell. I don't remember having any homeboys named James. But why is this nigga obsessed with me? Have I fucked his old lady or something? Dammit what other James do I know around here other than my dead father and Dr. James? Oh shit could it be. His voice did sound a little familiar.*"

"Detective, Detective Johnson!" a voice shouted. Zone out, Leroy immediately snapped out of it. "Oh I'm sorry Captain I was day dreaming about something what's up?"

"Well it seems that you were right about Mr. Brooks not being the killer."

"Why you say that?"

"Cause a man reported this morning seeing someone fitting his description being forced into an abandoned crack house." Cox laid a piece of paper on Leroy's desk. "Here is his name and address. I need you to talk to him and see what you can find out," Cox said. Leroy grabbed the piece of paper and stuck it in his pocket. "What do you think this mean?" Leroy asked. "It looks like the killer is trying to knock off loose ends and we can't let him get away, not this time," Cox added. "What if you wrong?" Leroy asked. "If so we'll continue as planned just keep an eye on Brooks and hope that the killer sticks his head out. But if not and Brooks is dead, it's going to be on your ass Leroy," Cox said.

"Why are you putting this on me?"

"Because it was your idea to let his black ass go remember."

"That's because he was not our killer."

"But he's involved," Cox quickly shot back. "Man whatever," Leroy stood up from his chair. "I'll go and see what this man knows and I get back with you later." Leroy grabs a few things off his desk and headed out the precinct without saying another word to Cox. While Cox just stood there with a hateful look on his face shaking his head.

Chapter 28

"Is that pussy free?"

"No but it's cheap."

They met in the bootlegger on Old Town Road in Ellenboro. She was glad that she didn't dress promiscuous. After several shots of liquor and a few beers they decided to get a room at the Holiday Inn.

They had been here before many times, licking each other up and down. "I've been wondering how you've been. I haven't seen you in a while what's up?" she said. "I've been busy with work. This bible killer shit got me going crazy. In fact I have to get back to the station soon."

"Some of the girls said they noticed five O' walking the streets tonight asking questions about that Surratt nigga, they working for you?"

"Yeah we think he was kidnapped from this area." Belinda sat in an overstuffed leather chair. Her shoes and socks were off. Hailey laid on the bed with only her t-shirt and panties on. "Is he the one they found behind the guardrail?"

"That's him, I've got a picture." Belinda held the photo for Hailey to see. She took it in her hand. "He was wearing a blue shirt and blue jeans when we found him." Hailey shook her head. "Damn, I think I have saw this little nigga. I have seen him somewhere before, I just can't remember…Ah… Wait! The last time Smoke and I were together he was getting into a car. I remember thinking how much I wanted to fuc --- well never mind." Belinda stirred excited. "What did you see?"

"A white Lincoln town car, I remember seeing that. And I think a bitch was driving."

"Do you remember anything else?" Belinda asked. Hailey leaned back against the pillows, sat up right and turned to her. Suddenly she thought about the white Lincoln, the female looking driver. "No that's all I can remember," she then turned on her nasty sluttish voice usually held for the customers, manipulative but whatever it took to get her pussy licked. She spread her legs open and ran her hand down her panties sticking her finger in and out her wet pussy. "Belinda please stay here and eat my wet pussy tonight."

"I'm supposed to be back at the station right now," she smiled. "Please just tonight, stay with me," her eyes begged. She had never seen this side of her. Hot, vulnerable, and trained to go. Hailey watched Belinda get up with a puzzled look on her face. She walked toward the light switch and turned it off. The darkness covered them. Hailey held her hands out and waited for her to lay on top of her. "I knew you couldn't resist this pussy."

.

<u>Chapter 29</u>

It was an old torn down apartment complex off Washington Avenue with a mixture of split level brick homes. Across the street from it, children's bicycles and torn up plastic toys were scattered all over the complex. One could count on at least three or four crack dealers standing in front of someone's apartment on any given Friday morning. Leroy pulled up in front of a section off apartment building with a man coming out heading to his van. He looked at Leroy getting out of his car. He stopped and waited. "I'm looking for Malcolm Kennedy, nick name Pacman." the man was wearing black jeans, timberland boots and a t-shirt with a Polo logo. He sized up Leroy quickly. "Are you the police or something nigga?" Leroy took out his badge. "District police Leroy Johnson is you Malcolm Kennedy?" he released his grip on his car keys and relaxed. "That's me," he said. "What's up?"

"I'm investigating a possible kidnapping of a Lewis Brooks. I understand that you left your name and address with one of our officers at the station to be contacted."

"Yeah but I never mentioned anyone being kidnapped."

"But you did mention someone being forced into an abandoned house fitting this description." Leroy took out a mug shot picture of Brooks and held it up in Pacman's face. "Is this the man you saw?"

"Yeah but what makes you think he's been kidnapped?"

"Because he can't be found," Leroy said. "Now tell me what you saw."

"Well check it, I was coming in late about five, my van," he pointed at the parked green Dodge Caravan. "Wouldn't start right away so I needed a jump off from my girl's car, anyways I called and said I'll be late, I parked in the lot and was walking inside when I saw these two niggaz, one of them had a gun at the other man's back forcing him into an abandon trap house," he looked around. "I'm telling you my nigga the man with the gun looked like something off of the tales of the crypt."

"What did the nigga with the gun look like? Can you describe him?"

"I told you the nigga looked crazy, he was tall with long white hair, and black as hell."

"Clothes?"

"He wore a suit, all black with a black and white neck tie."

"Did you see what they were riding in?"

"A white car I'm pretty sure it was white but I don't know what type it was. I mean I would know if I've got a closer look, but I really wasn't paying attention. I was in a rush to get to work. I was late as hell so the only reason I paid any attention was because the nigga looked weird, well that and the fact it was five in the morning, usually don't see much of anyone going in and out at that time." Leroy scribbled in his notebook.

"Did you notice anything else about the man?" Pacman thought for a moment and put his hand to his chin.

"There was one other thing," he looked around again. "I didn't tell the officer at the station. I didn't think of it until after I spoke to him, and I wasn't going to call back." Leroy moved in closer. "It probably doesn't mean shit anyway." Leroy didn't respond. "When they both went into the house I heard someone holler."

"Like who?"

"I don't know it sounded like it came from inside the house." Leroy's eyebrows traveled up. "You mean to tell me that you saw all this and waited a whole hour to report it to the police?"

"Man I'm no snitch!" Pacman exploded. "And the only reason why I reported it is because I didn't want it on my conscious knowing that somebody was in trouble." Leroy held his composure. "I understand Mr. Kennedy thank you for your help," Leroy shook Malcolm's hand and headed to his car. "That's it?"

"That's it," Leroy said as he got in his car. "And one more thing!" he shouted back at Malcolm. "If your consciousness decides it wants to snitch about anything else you know where to find me."

Chapter 30

Leroy had just came in the house when the phone rang. He rushed to the phone and picked it up. "Hello?"

"What's up Leroy this is Belinda?"

"What's up? Where have you been all night?" Leroy asked. "I've been trying to reach you."

"Didn't get home until -- well early this morning, needed to talk to you about the case." she related Hailey's story leaving out her personnel relationship with her. It was a part of her life which she wasn't particularly proud of. "Belinda," Leroy said. "From what you're saying and what the eye witness told me the white Lincoln is the connection and a possible female accomplice that puts a new spin on things."

Chapter 31

Even with the door open Marie Johnson's house faintly smelled like pig's feet and ass. She sat in front of the TV eating a Big Mac with fries and a coke, piercing the TV with the lightest brown eyes in the world. Leroy sat across from her in a black leather recliner waiting patiently for his mom's favorite TV program to go off. "I've seen this one before, it's a rerun from last week." Marie grabbed the remote from the coffee table and turned the channel. "So have you come up with any new leads on the case? I'm sorry I haven't got back with you on what we were talking about yesterday."

"Oh, that's okay I just came by to clear my head a little," Leroy lied about the real reason why he was there. He figured that his mother may be able to give him a better in-depth profile of the killer giving the fact that she took up criminal justice for two years and interviewed several death row inmates for a journalist try out program. "But since you brought it up I need your option on something."

"What's that?" she asked. "When you called me yesterday I was working up a profile sheet. Leroy reached over and grabbed his suit case beside the couch that his mother was sitting on and took out a chart sheet along with a synopsis of each killing and laid it on the coffee table in front of his mom. She looked down at the chart sheet and back up at Leroy. "Don't just sit there watching me read, see what else is on TV." he grabbed the remote and turns the TV off. "Why did you turn it off?" she snapped. "You can't read and watch television too." she realized that he had a point and continued reading without saying another word, after 15 minutes of silence she finally spoke. "Son my opinion is that this guy gets his excitement from exerting complete control over the life of his victims, the kick is from knowing that he has the power to do whatever he wishes to another human being. Don't get me wrong son he's not crazy he knows exactly what he's doing, he knows all the rules of society but chooses to ignore them. He lives by his own law," she looked out her window at a pit bull barking at a man walking up the street then back at Leroy. "He personalizes the victims and has controlled conversations with them."

"Is it before or after he kills them?" Leroy asked. "What do you think?" she snapped back with a disappointed look on her face. "Of course it's going to be before he kills them, you can't socialize with the dead."

"Well the man on psycho did."

"Didn't I say the man wasn't crazy and besides that's movie stuff this is real," she looked again at Leroy's notes. "High IQ, the writing style of his letters indicates good education, skilled worker, not ghetto, I'd say he makes a good living. He's socially competent, good negotiator, good at parties. People think he's nerdy and clever, possibly not good looking but dresses nicely, maybe never been with a pretty woman in his life."

"Well speaking of women what's your opinion of his female accomplices?"

"That's a hard one, I don't know much about women killers only from what I've read in novels, I'd say women in this type of business are thrill seekers, and they will have sex with the male victims while he watches. He might even participate but I don't think this is the case here, what I do think is that they play the game together, they share the thrill of catching, controlling, killing and…." she hesitated. "Making you look stupid that's the most important thing to them, playing you. It's a major component of their power grip I can see that. There is something else you should know. This type often keeps records like prizes or trophies, he may videotape the murders take pictures of them, and keep notes something like that. I remember watching a movie on lifetime were the killer videotape the deaths of his victims and download it on his computer disc. Your guy I would guess keeps a record of everything he has done to his victims."

"I wouldn't doubt that, but the question is what does he want from me?"

"He wants to beat you, control you mentally that is. He want stop until you stoop to his level, watch you go back to prison and lose everything you have." Leroy stood up from the recliner looking down at his mother with a slight smile on his face. "Trust me mom that's not going to happen." grabbing is stuff from off the coffee table and putting it back into his suit case, he leaned over and kiss is mother on the cheek. "I appreciate!"

"Oh no problem," she replied. Leroy started toward the door when suddenly she spoke again causing him to turn his attention to her. "Oh don't forget to bring Kametica by to see me Sunday, I'm thinking about making her a banana pudding and some apple pie after church."

"I won't mom," replied Leroy. "Just don't forget about finding out that last name for me," Leroy said tossing a large yellow envelop on the couch beside his mom. "What's this?"

"Some more letters from the killer, check them out they may be useful.

Chapter 32

He pulled his white Lincoln behind two large green trash cans that sat next to an eight-foot fence that surrounded the apartment complex, trying not to be seen he quickly bounced up the stairs, two at a time delivering a dope package to a Pam Brown apartment 6D, for a instance he halt in mid step wondering if he had locked the car door. "*Hell nobody is going to fuck with my stuff,*" he thought. He laughed it off and continued. He spied the top step and with a jump like Michael Jordan made it to the landing. He wasn't even tired as his big timberland boot hit the ground with a thud that echoed through the hallway, trying to remember if the apartment was on the left hand side or the right he guessed that it was on the right and was correct. "*That's what's up,*" he mutters as he knocked on the door with three quick loud jabs. No answer. He checked his watch and looked around over his shoulder impatiently hopping from one foot to the other, he hears shoes on a wooden floor occupied by a female voice singing Mary J. "I'm coming, I'm coming," a few more steps. "Who is it?"

"It's me."

"Me who?" she replied. The peephole opened, realizing who it was she took in his enthusiastic eager face, hopping up and down and his fingers tapping the bag of powder. "About time," she said as she opened the door. "Where's Lewis he…" before she could finish her sentence the bag of dope fell as a hand lunged for her wrist. She jerked her arm but couldn't break free, she backed into the apartment and the two collide in a scuffle, his foot kicked the door closed behind them, she saw his lips tighten, his eyes widen as if he had smoked a rock. He took out a small syringe from his shirt pocket and pulled the protective cover with his teeth and spit it out. He pulled on her arm, squeezing until her swelled veins showed through her ashy brown skin. The needle slide into her forearm, she collapsed immediately in his arms.

With the body hidden in the trunk of his car he drove around the hood several times to make sure nobody was watching him pull his car in his back yard. He would wait until dark before he carried her into the house, the drug would last a few more hours at least, now all he wanted to do was get out of them baggy jeans and hoodie and change himself back into Dr. Spears and smoke a blunt.

<u>Chapter 33</u>

Tina Walker had just finished typing in the name Leroy Johnson Mecklenburg Detective on her home computer keyboard by using the search engine, she scanned through the database for any stories containing the name Detective Johnson that also contained the word Mecklenburg, in this way she was sure to find material about this ex-con name Leroy Johnson turned police and not some asshole with the same name who made the news because he was shot in the face by some crazy stick up kid. The screen blinked three times before showing that it had located four stories. Tina pressed the print key and waited. Ever since her encounter with Johnson at the Brooks house Tina couldn't stand the man, it wasn't a deep hatred but more like she just didn't care much for him as a person, knowing he was the only man standing between her and access to the killer. Tina thought that if she could give the killer some dirt on Johnson then the killer might be willing to do an interview with her. As the printer shot paper Tina thought how she would set the kill up so that he wouldn't be seen, how she would manipulate the camera to hide his face and yet let the people of Mecklenburg see that this man has a reason for his actions. He has killed three people and will more likely kill again but what is his reason for killing these people? We'll find out soon enough. Tina grabbed the printed paper and began reading. The later stories about the current crimes were of no interest. Tina looked through them and immediately threw them away, suddenly she spotted a story in the Mecklenburg post six years ago about a detective who was allowed to investigate a murder case involving his brother, a convicted drug dealer and gang member, the story was small and brief only a couple of pictures of the defendant and his full name and address. Tina turned to the computer again and type in Tyrone Johnson and the word murder. Blink, one story. *"Gang member convicted In Dodge City murder"* By Rose Willkie: Mecklenburg Post Staff Writer.

After four days of deliberation a jury convicted an African-American gang member of the murder of a drug addict whose body was found behind a bootlegger in Dodge City. Amy Shakespeare 30 of Ellenboro was found dead March'15th in a dumpster behind a house where alcohol and drugs were being sold. Police said that Tyrone Johnson 31 was the last person with Amy before her death, medical examiner's office said Shakespeare died from contaminated cocaine. Johnson pleads innocent to the charges saying he had met Amy in a club and they agreed to meet later in Dodge City. He testified that he was in Dodge City to sell Amy some dope but she refuse to buy from him, saying that his rocks were too small and that she was waiting on someone with a better deal. At his trial Leroy try to give an explanation for how Amy died. He said that Ms. Shakespeare was seen buying drugs from a Hispanic man driving a black ford escort, the same escort that was confiscated by police days after the murder on Highway 74 in which rat poison was found in a small bag inside the car. He claimed she was given rat poison instead of crack cocaine. Leroy denied knowing that Shakespeare was a junkie with a history of five arrests for possession of crack cocaine, police say they were not able to verify Leroy story of an unknown assailant despite the long three month investigation that included the victim's family and friends. At the time of the investigation Detective Leroy Johnson was assigned to the homicide squad but was not permitted to actively pursue the case because of his relationship with the suspect, however Leroy voluntarily took a leave of absence to pursue his own investigation.

Homicide Capt. David Cox said. "The police department does not condone or support his actions and that they have no authority over any of the offices during leave. We understand Detective Johnson's personal interest in this matter and we sympathize with him."

Johnson's lawyer Kent Edward said. "He will appeal the conviction." which carries 25 years to life in prison. Edward will appeal on the grounds that the prosecution introduced past convictions in which to picture his client as a menace to society and a violent gang member that needed to be taken off the streets.

Tina highlighting the story in red marker, she plans to tell the killer when he calls. "Hi Tina, do you know who this is?"

"Yeah I think so."

"What do you mean you think so?" the voice shot back hatefully. "I mean you sound different," she said almost dropping the phone. The voice was deep, clear and calm. "I decided to have the interview, we'll hook up tonight to set up the time and day is that straight with you Tina?"

"Hell yeah that's straight with me."

"That's what's up, met me at the Waffle House on Crestview Lane 8:30 PM."

Waffle House, Tina didn't know that Mecklenburg had a Waffle House. "Okay," the phone went dead and Tina reached into her pocket for her GPS.

Chapter 34

"The Waffle House huh? You are kidding me?"

"Nope, you want to hear it yourself?" Belinda said holding a disc in her hand. "Nah I believe you I just didn't think this guy was still calling her," Leroy stood up from his desk. "Did they say what time they were going to meet?"

"If I can remember I think 8:30."

"Seems like good timing to me, let's get KT ass in on the action."

"Okay." Belinda made a quick phone call to KT's office and left word on his answer machine and turn to Leroy who was still at his desk flipping through a black tail magazine. "Are you ready?"

"I don't know I may have to take a moment to get right."

"What do you mean get right," looking curious down at the black tailed magazine on Leroy desk. "Oh that," she said catching on to the joke. "Stop playing and come on."

"Alright I'm coming just give me a minute to make a phone call."

"Hello this is Sgt. Lincoln."

"Yeah this is Detective Johnson is you busy?"

"No why?"

"I need you to help me secure the Waffle House on Crestview."

"What there's going to be a party at the Waffle House?"

"Shit I wish."

"Well what do you got?"

"The man they call the Bible killer."

"You sure it's him?"

"I'm positive. So are you going to help me or what?"

"It depends."

"Depends on what?"

"It depends on who else is helping you," Joseph pauses and then continues. "You know Mecklenburg is not my district and if it gets word that I'm helping you secure some damn Waffle House my white ass is screw."

"Man you don't have to worry about that my brother, it's just going to be me, Belinda and KT you know I don't mess with that many people at this station."

"Well okay, you can count me in, so when is all this going down?"

"Tonight we're meeting at my house at four O'clock for a briefing," he pauses. "Hold on for a minute." Leroy didn't hang up the phone he just pressed the button on his cell phone for another line. He called KT to let him know that Sgt. Joseph will be coming a long and that they will be meeting at his house at four. KT responded, saying he'll be there but he will be a little late.

Leroy paced the living room floor while the three waiting for KT to get there, walkie-talkie squawked in Joseph hand. Belinda went to open the door for KT who had just arrived.

"Sources tell us that the Bible killer plans to be at the Waffle House tonight." Leroy tossed a photo of Tina Walker on the coffee table. "He's going to meet this woman and we all know who she is, she's the TV reporter named Tina Walker and she has a special interest in this case."

 "Reminds me of my ex-wife always in the middle of something," said Joseph. The four laugh it off while Leroy continued. "Now check it, Tina isn't involved in the killings so she's not to be arrested unless she gets in the way, keep in mind however that she is our biggest connection to the killer. We don't want to scare the hell out of her. I don't have to tell you that if this guy gets the idea that we are following her he won't come." Joseph cleared his throat. "Do you know what the killer looks like?"

"Only a general description based on what I have gathered up, I believe the killing is a black man who is probably in his late 30s or early 40s, there's also word that he may have one or two female accomplice's, the only description I have on one is," he pause for a second and glance over at Joseph. "She's white with a nice body." Joseph grunted and smiled. Leroy waited a moment and continued. "He or she might be driving a white Lincoln so that means that I want this bitch tailed as soon as she's near the Waffle House, now the sheets I've just gave y'all is a description of her POV and that of the TV station unmark cars, I believe she'll be driving her black Jeep so KT I'm going to need you inside the Waffle House and you," pointing his finger at Joseph. "I'm going to need you on the roof."

"Come on Leroy, why do I have to get on the roof?" Joseph asked. "You don't want to be seen doing cop stuff in Mecklenburg do you?" Joseph scratched his head knowing Leroy was right. "Well no."

"Alright then," replied Leroy. "Now Belinda you going to be on the ground with me surrounding the area, we will also need night scopes." he jabbed the table with his pen as to express that he was done explaining the details of the operation, he glanced over at Belinda who nodded back. "What are we looking for Leroy?" Joseph asked. "A verbal meeting or it may be a handoff I don't know for sure, that's why we can't jump on the first person Tina talks to because it might be just a nobody trying to get fresh. So y'all just be on point and be in position by seven O'clock."

At 7:15.Dr. James Spear opened up his closet door, searching under some old empty boxes and shoes he found his white apron. "There you are," he mutters to himself. He rolled up the old smelly garment and placed it in a plastic bag. He then crawled beneath his king size bed and grabbed a set of black high top boots, he placed the boots and the plastic bag into an oversize book bag that said FUBU, looking at the bag he thought what else could he be missing. He snapped his finger. *"Oh that's it,"* he said to himself quickly snatching a ball cap off a shelf in his bed room. "Thanks Mike I knew it would come in handy." flopped the hat on his head, he swung the book bag over his shoulder and headed out.

Tina Walker thought about her dress for quite a while and finally settled on blue jeans, a plain black shirt and tennis shoes. She wondered how the killer would look or how he would approach her, would he just come right up and say. *"What's up bitch I'm the Bible killer,"* or would he hide behind the restaurant and call her out by name. But whatever the case maybe she was safe knowing she had a 357 stuffed in her purse so he better not dare make a move on her she thought. Tina took the computer print outs and stuffed them in her pocket book, going over in her head what she had rehearsed about Johnson's brother, the dead crack head woman, the conviction and the long criminal record that came out during the trial. The dirt is good enough to trade maybe good enough for an on camera interview.

Leroy sat patiently in the passenger side of a dark blue Buick with South Carolina tags. Mecklenburg police often registered their undercover cars out of state and it always trip Leroy out how many times it fooled him during his days as a street hustler, despite the fact that unmarked cars telegraphed their presence with cheap hubcaps that police agencies bought. Usually there will be an antenna sticking out of the truck lid.

It was 7:50, Leroy and Belinda positioned their car pass the front of the Waffle House on Washington Avenue a divide highway. They couldn't let no one see them pulling up in front of the restaurant it was too risky for either of them to actually be in the mix. Tina knew what they both look like and chances are the killer did too.

KT walked around inside the place as a customer. The restaurant wasn't as busy as usually only on

Fridays and Saturday nights when customers would come inside and mingle as if the restaurant was a nightclub, music jumping, little young niggaz standing around the place selling hard, bitches arguing and fighting over their baby daddies, it became a weekend tradition. People who live near the restaurant frequently complained about the constant fighting and loud music that goes on every weekend at the place. A liquor house stood across the street from it as well. During the day drunks would walk in the restaurant carrying sandwich bags, begging the customers for their scraps from their plates and stealing the tip's from off the tables.

The Waffle House was starting to get pack at 8:05 as dope dealers competed with each other on the corner as they try to get rid of as much crack as they could so they wouldn't have to re-up at midnight, during which business is booming for hustlers in the hood. Scared white customers took their food to go

as niggaz poured inside the Waffle House as if TI

was there.

It was during this time that Tina Walker appeared,

she didn't fit into this type of crowd of niggaz,

chanting rap songs, and beaten on tables and

demanding the waiters to take their orders. She

walked about as if she was Queen of England and

everybody else was beneath her.

Joseph spotted her as soon as she got out of her

car and into the Waffle House. The radio

conveyed her every move, cameras recorded any

person coming near and no matter where she was

James Spear was watching her too. But nobody

paid his ass any attention. He was dressed in the

same manner as other workers, white apron black

boots the whole nine, he began cleaning up the

area loaning frozen meats into the deep freezer and hosing down walkways.

Leroy and Belinda felt very left out who resigned to listen to the action on the radio trying to imagine where Tina was exactly, and what she was doing based on Joseph and KT's reports. Leroy resisted the urge to pick up the walkie-talkie and guide his people in the ghetto art of surveillance. He knew the two were qualified and handpicked by him but he still felt tempted to ask if they saw anything unusual, he wanted to ask bad as hell. "Fuck!" he couldn't resist, he picked up the radio anyway.

"What's Tina doing now? Have she'd talk to anyone yet? Tell me what the fuck is going on man?"

On the roof from across the street Joseph saw something. "Subject appears to be ordering something to eat," he said into the walkie-talkie.

Tina looked at the menu. "What is this?" she asked a Jamaican waiter. The man who spoke broken English look down at her and said. "Yes m'on very good pine apple egg omelet very, very good you want?"

"No thank you," replies Tina.

KT who was dressed in street clothes picked out his fro and tucks his earpiece in his sock. He walked slowly to Tina's table. "Don't know what you want to eat?" the Jamaican waiter continued to show eagerness to take her order, noticing KT he looked at him. "Do you want pine apple omelet m'on?"

"No thank you bro, I'm still trying to decide."

"Alright m'on," he said quickly then turned back to Tina. "Want steak? Steak is good m'on."

I'm good," she replied as she stood up from her table, purse in hand. "Excuse me I have to go to the restroom."

 Minutes later a bunch of street punk's scampered their way inside the Waffle House. "This muthafucka is pack man."

"What's up my nigga?" one of the young boys wearing a red scarf around his head hollered. As he gave dap to a guy who was sitting at the table next to the entrance door. The sound of 50 cent could be heard from outside. The eight young boys responded by dancing to the music, bobbin their heads and waving their arms back and forth, few of the boys began dancing towards the cash register. Then all of a sudden the happy mood change as the boy with the red scarf around his head pulled out his pistol and pointed it at the lady at the cash register. "Stop tripping nigga!" "Does it look like I'm tripping bitch? So let me get that paper." his home boys boost him up, other customers scattered as someone screamed about a gun. Leroy tensed up when he heard reports of the commotion.

"Damn them dumb ass niggaz is going to mess it up Belinda." the radio went silent and Leroy knew what that meant, he called to KT inside. "Where is she?" no response. "Dammit KT where is she?" "Last seen coming from the ladies bathroom," KT said. "Her car is still here," said Joseph from the roof. "Then she has to be here we need to get visual on her before the police get here," Leroy said. Six minutes passed. "See anything Joseph?" Leroy asked. "Nothing but the police is heading this way." one minute pass. "Fuck it let's do this

Belinda," Leroy push the radio button. "I want the bitch found now, so do whatever y'all have to do." KT and Joseph were startled, they didn't know how to react as Joseph immediately got off the roof, while KT began flashing his badge around demanding people to move. "Move, move get out of the way move please." the police came in fast. "Everyone freeze!" an officer said. "Who's checking the back?" Leroy said. "Got it," Joseph said. "All clear," he adds. "What the fuck," said the boy with the red scarf around his head, when a white officer elbowed him to the floor. "Is this the nigger with the gun?"

"You don't have to be that rough!" shouted a woman in the back. "He didn't do anything, he was just playing."

"Yeah my nigga give that redneck ass cop that play gun." Leroy couldn't wait any longer, him and Belinda jumped out the vehicle and ran over towards the Waffle House. "Have you seen a man and woman leaving on foot?" he asked a man picking up cans around park cars. "Nah," the man responded. "Sure haven't," he added. Leroy and Belinda decided to split up and check the vehicles, when the two departed, the man continued to pick cans. He paused, wiped his forehead with a handkerchief and shuffle over to a large brown trash can. He lift the large black lid about several inches and peeked inside. "Hope you're not too hot and stuffy in there Tina," he said dropping the lid back down.

Chapter 35

"Welcome to my hide out," James Spear announced to his company. Tina Walker and Pam

Brown sat on the same side of a long handmade wooden table. James sat at the head and Eve at the opposite end. The table was messy with old magazines and dirty silver ware. "I guess you didn't expect this Tina, I hate having to extricate you in such a way, but I apologize but either way you ask for this, you desperately wanted to know about the great James Spear." he looked over at Pam. "I wish you could have worked for me a little longer you was such a good employee of my, I'm going to miss screwing you," he added.

Pam Brown's eyes were dead, her body sat hunched barely holding her head up, although hidden from Tina's view by the table she was tied to her chair by a small cable wire. She stared briefly at James, her face trying to understand his words then retreated to her front and center dazed condition.

"Well," James started to continue. "What the hell is I'm doing here?" Tina asked. "What are you doing? Let me go," she started to get up but found her right foot chained to the floor. "What the..."

 "Tina baby this chill, this will all be over soon enough, and oh yeah, I read the papers in your pocket book, were they supposed to be for me?" Tina didn't respond. "Tell me it wasn't, you think I don't know all about Detective Johnson and his bitch ass brother? Please don't play with my intelligence woman."

Tina felt her heart beating faster and faster, her breathing came in a gasps, she thought she was going to hyperventilate. James noticed. "Just relax Tina no one is going to touch you, see I can't have you fucking this up for me that's the reason I have your foot chained to the floor. I can't have you running off to the police now can I?" he said harshly then smiled.

Eve finally spoke. "Tina," she said softly rubbing her hand on her breast. "James is telling the truth no one is going to hurt you." Tina sat back, she tugged on her leg a second time to make sure the chain was secure. Then she watched as Eve and James without saying anything walk into an open bedroom and shut the door. "Hey!" Tina shouted after them. "What about us?" she looked across at Pam. "You're all right?" she touched her face trying to snap her out of her dazed. "Hey!" James stormed into the room approaching Tina with fast speed. He slapped her in the face. "What the fuck are you doing? What did I tell you about touching her you stupid black bitch?"

"I'm sorry I was just seeing if she was alright."

"I don't won't to hear any excuses just keep your damn hands off of her." Tina was so shocked by the outburst she pissed on herself. "Do I make myself clear?" James shouted. "Do I?" Smack! I've had just about enough out of you; you're going to be punished bitch," he stormed into the other room. "We got to get the fuck out of here," Tina said to Pam. She pulled on the chain with both hands. "These niggaz are crazy and…" Tina stopped talking when she saw James return, this time with Eve. "Looked at her," James said. "She thinks she got all the sense." Tina saw the madness in James eyes. Eve calmly walked over by Tina just beyond arm reach. "Why did you touch her? Tell me why?" she said. "All I did was try to help her wiped her face I…"
"What did I tell you?" James shouted. "The bitch thinks she's slick, she's got to pay."

"I'm afraid I can't help you Tina, please forgive me," Eve said softly. "What are y'all planning on doing to me all I did was… please don't hurt me, please." that was her last words before being dragged to the bottom of the basement.

It was after midnight when the four assembled at headquarters. "What the hell happened tonight?" Leroy's asked as he paced back and forth across the room. "What the hell happened out there?" nobody answered. "I'll tell you what the fuck happened, we let that nigga get away and our bait is missing that's what happened." KT spoke after the echoes of Leroy's voice faded. "It's my bad, I lost her in the commotion with those kids, I messed up what else can I say?" the others in the room concurred under their breaths. "We're not going to get anywhere by worrying about who did what," Belinda said. "While it's still fresh in our minds let's go over what happened." each of them in turn told exactly what they saw and heard, it ended with Joseph saying that the police was on the premises, and that the Waffle House was shut down for 12 minutes after Tina was out of sight and the killer or she could have left in any car or van that left during those 12 minutes without being checked. "Anything else," Leroy asked? "I want to know who was behind the ruckus because obviously this person was creating a decoy for the killer in order for him to get away. So KT I want them employees question tonight, carry a picture of Tina, check and see if anyone remember seeing her."

"I don't eat at the Waffle House but I'll take care of it," said Belinda. "Y'all got my cell phone number call me when you know something." the two bounced and Belinda walked over to Leroy who was gathering his papers. "We had that nigga Belinda, we fucking had him."

"Do you think he knew that her phone was tapped, knew we were waiting?"

"Hell no, not unless he saw us and I don't think he did, I think he was planning to grab Tina all along. It's like I said he caused that disturbance with the kids as insurance against people in the Waffle House and not us."

"You think so?" Belinda asked.

"I know so."

"Go home Leroy I'll talk to you tomorrow."

<u>Chapter 36</u>

Over the next few days reports felled on Leroy desk back to back, he tried to dispatch them as quickly as possible by putting in extra hours, this was his way of

trying to make up for the fuck up at the Waffle

House. A check of license tags showed that a blue

and white truck which had arrived at the restaurant

before 8:30 was reported stolen two hours before the

stake out. It was found the following morning

abandoned at the East Rutherford High School and

was sent directly to impound where Joseph looked

over it.

Leroy was sitting at his desk when Joseph walked in

eating a pack of M&M's. "What's up Joseph?" Leroy

said. "Now tell me about the truck." Joseph explained

how the truck was so junky with beer cans and old

newspapers. "The owner came to the impound to see

if anything important was taken, nothing had been

taken but something was added, he didn't know how

a pair of Air Ones had gotten there. They weren't his, I've gotten the shoes but I don't know what to do with them I can't fit them," said Joseph. "They are nice too."

"Why would this guy leave a pair of Air Ones behind?"

"I don't know maybe he had an extra set of shoes and forgot that he left them in the truck." Leroy rubbed his chin. "Well I guess you're right." the two went silent for a couple of seconds and then Joseph spoke. "So if there's not anything else you need me to do with the truck I like to give it back to the owner a-sap."

"No problem," said Leroy. "But keep the shoes I may need them." the phone rang and it was KT. "I found them niggaz who started that mess at the Waffle House and guess what? This shit is going to trip you out, they said somebody came up to them when they were hanging out on the block on Wales Drive and gave them an ounce of hard to crash the Waffle House. The only thing they had to do was to play like they were robbing the place so that it would cause a commotion, is that not crazy?"

"Yup, could they describe the guy?"

"It wasn't a dude it was a white girl, said she was thick as hell wearing tight baby phat jeans." Leroy wasn't surprise he knew exactly who that bitch was. "What was she driving?"

"Don't know, just gave them the dope and told them to bounce, they were drunk as hell at the time."

"Any of the dope left?"

"They said they sold it all but who knows. I ran into Belinda at the Waffle House she said to tell you that showing the pictures of Tina around the area was a waste of time except for that Jamaican waiter, but she's got a few more people to talk too. Hasn't come into work yet but she just wanted to let you know what was up."

"I appreciate that," Leroy spun around when he heard Capt. Cox voice. "Detective Johnson someone is here to see you." Cox presented Jimmy Luster general manager of Eyewitness News. Leroy and Mr. Luster had spoken on the phone the day after he told Luster that Tina's vehicle was left outside the Waffle House after it had closed, and that a few people had spoken to her before her disappearance. Leroy didn't say anything about Tina schedule meeting with the killer. Luster was dressed in a dark blue conservative business suit with a light blue necktie; his face was very dark for a white man even though Leroy figured he was mixed with a little nigga. Leroy noticed that

Luster must be a little gay too, because he twitched when he walked. "What can I do for you Mr. Luster?"

"I'm sorry but I don't have anything new to tell you about Walker's disappearance."

"Is there some place we can talk privately Detective?"

"Yeah follow me; is it all right for the Capt. to come?"

"Sure," Leroy places his hand on Luster arm as if to guide him. "Are you alright?"

"Of course, it's just that... well nothing like this has ever happen before. I mean I've been doing this job for 30 years I've covered the Rae Carruth and the Michael Peterson murders, I've seen people shot right in front of me but nothing like this."

"I know man come on inside," said Leroy holding the door open to the interrogation room. "Can I get you something to drink?" ask Cox. "No I'm okay." Luster placed a DVD disc on the table.

"This was sent to me today, here is the envelope I brought it with me just in case you need it," Luster took a deep breath and continued. "I played it on my laptop and it's sick, you'll see," Luster sat back. "We encouraged Walker to work on the Bible killer story, we really thought it would be good for the station and for Walker's career, we didn't think it would go to this level. Walker always told us that she wasn't scared and that she could take care of herself. We were wrong Detective."

"I've seen this over and over Amanda but I'll like to know what you think?" Leroy said. "I don't know Leroy I really don't have the time."
"Please!" Leroy said presenting a puppy face. "Well since you asked politely I guess so," Amanda Rose took the CD and inserted it into the DVD player in the conference room near her laboratory, she walked to

a seat next to Leroy and fibbed with the remote until the TV screen went from black to color. The three were nude on a wooden floor, the wall behind them was light brown, Lewis Brooks lay on top of Tina Walker while sweat dripped down the side of Pam Brown faced as she sucks on Lewis big black balls. "I love these black ass nuts," she said savagely. Lewis began hitting the pussy, Tina showed no emotion, she held onto his back with only the slightest grip, as Pam threw her head back off from between Lewis and Tina legs and crawled over to the other end of them. She then put her pussy in Lewis mouth. "Eat my wet pussy nigga," she said. Without any hesitation he said. "Whatever you say baby," he looked up at Pam and back down at Tina as he continued fucking vigorously, faintly a voice off camera whispered. "Yeah fuck them bitches' nigga."

"Damn this pussy is good, why want you stop smoking dope and be my bitch?"

"Hell yeah that's right," the voice whispered. Taking his mouth off of Pam's pussy again, he cleared his throat and spoke slowly, sounds of talking could be heard from the background. "Run away with me, your pimp will never know."

"He knows," a voice seemed to come from Pam but her lips weren't moving, they were parted but motionless. "I think he's right Pam," said Tina moaning and groaning still fucking, her face full of pain and pleasure. "I'll kill the nigga," and Lewis face strained. "Damn I'm about too... I can't hold it... it's...

"No!" the voice whispered. "Don't nut yet."

Chapter 37

Suddenly the screen went black, the TV made a raspy noise. Amanda pressed the off button on the DVD and everything went quite for a moment, she and Leroy sat in the dark without talking for about 10 seconds or so when Amanda got up and turned the light on. "Well Leroy what kinda of shit was that?"

"I don't know but every time I look at it makes me horny."

 "Be for real Leroy who are those three and where in the hell did you get that CD?" Leroy explained about the Lewis and the Tina Walker kidnappings. He said he didn't have a clue about the other woman in the video but he knew for a fact that the CD came from the killer. "Turn the DVD back on while I get a notepad I want to check it out again," Amanda said. As they sat in the dark the light of the screen flickering into their eyes, Leroy saw disgust in Amanda's face turn into one of concentration, when it was over she had filled up four small pages with notes. "Here's what I think. Tina and Lewis and whoever that other woman was, were acting. The three were probably high on something, it's obvious they were reading some kinda of script." Leroy nodded. "So if that was the killer in the background, the male voice we heard I'd say he was forcing them to act out a special scene. Maybe a fantasy of his or something from his past, what exactly I don't know."

Amanda stood up and walked around the room, she looked at Leroy. "But the problem is it may be nothing."

"So you're saying that there is no significance in this, is that supposed to help me?"

"Well you ask for my opinion and I told you."

"I understand -- assuming it was something from his past or whatever, why would he act it out?"

"Two reasons," Amanda rolled up her sleeves. "One by playing it out physically so that maybe he could come to grips with whatever happened in his past or two by acting it out, he may think he can change the outcome at least in his mind by having the actors change what really happened."

 "Kinda like trying to get rid of a bad dream?"

"Exactly, it's quite the remedy these days for psychos." Leroy thought about his brother crazy dreams and about Amy. "He may have a relationship with this woman and something happened to her."

"What about the… I'll kill the nigga stuff do you think he killed her pimp?"

"Don't know he might have or it might be part of the dream he's recasting. Maybe he wants to kill him-whoever the person is."

"How does this have to do with him killing all these niggaz?"

"I'm guessing it gives him a sense of power and control which he didn't have over her."

"That shit don't make any sense why would he want to control a bunch of drug dealers and gang members?"

"Maybe this person was more than just a pimp, he could've been a dealer himself and by killing these hoodlums was his way of releasing his hate for the pimp that controlled the woman he loved."

"That could explain why he brought in an outsider unfortunately big black Lewis couldn't hold back, she must had some snapper." Amanda glanced at Leroy with a slight disappointed look on her face, noticing this Leroy quickly corrected himself. "I'm sorry I meant to say why would he send this mess to Jimmy Luster?" Amanda thought for a second. "For publicity, he wants the media to know that he has their number one news lady Tina Walker and that there's not a damn thing they can do to save her."

"I believe he also knew they would send it to me and that I'd be sitting somewhere spending all my time and energy trying to figure it out." Amanda put down her pen and looked over at Leroy. "He sure has you not knowing if you are coming or going."

"It sure seems that way Amanda, it sure seems that way."

Chapter 38

"This shit is really getting old Leroy and it's making me and the whole damn police department look bad."

"I feel what you're saying Capt., but isn't that the news lady Tina Walker?" an officer asked, cutting into the conversation. "Yeah it's her."

"Who's the other two?" Leroy waited a moment to respond. "The man's name is Lewis Brooks, I have no idea who she is." the three were standing on the railroad tracks behind Cones Mills one of the last remaining industrial plants in Mecklenburg, their backs facing the massive traffic that lead to the mall and courthouse. In the distance the Wachovia Bank was reflecting a rising sun. "When did the call come in?" Leroy asked as he studied the three naked bodies. "Around 3 O'clock this morning said some homeless man found them," said the officer. Leroy bent down closer to the three bodies that were frozen on top of each other, their heads were facing the same direction, their arms were fully extended spread-crucifixion style with hands clasped tightly, wrists bound with cable wire.

Leroy knew he was going to have to kill this nigga, no doubt about that he thought. He stood up looking at the oncoming traffic from the railroad tracks when Belinda appeared from the opposite direction trying to catch her breath. "Boy! That's a hell of a hump," she spotted the dead bodies. "Damn! This nigga isn't playing is he?" Cox glanced over at Belinda trying to make sense of her statement, he started to make a scene but realized that she's been hanging around Leroy to long and decided not to but instead said, "What's up?" Belinda greeted him and pulled out a pack of Newport's from her purse, she punched a hole in the pack with her fingernail and proceeded to take out a cigarette never taking her eyes off the dead bodies. "This shit is getting crazy Leroy I be glad when we catch this bastard," she said lighting up her cigarette. Belinda attempted to try to change the subject about the situation but fell on deaf ears when Leroy didn't respond. Belinda shrugged and tossed her cigarette on the ground away from the scene and began videotaping the area, a minute later she was done. "All yours now," she said to Leroy after she turned off her video camera. Leroy didn't budge, he just stood there thinking about what Amanda said. He may had a relationship with this woman and something happen to her. "Go ahead Leroy I'm finished!" Belinda repeated. Leroy walked towards the dead bodies very slowly. "*Look nigga you can't play me I know* exactly *what you're trying to do*," he said to himself. He snapped on some latex gloves and proceeded to unwrap one set of cable wire, he dropped it in a plastic sandwich bag that the officer held open, and then the other set carefully unwinding, dropping it in another bag. Standing up Leroy motioned to Belinda who was discussing something with Capt. Cox. "Can you not wait until the medical examiners get here?" Belinda asked putting on gloves. "Nah, so help me out will you?" the bodies made a funny noise when they lifted Lewis by his stiff legs off the two women and slid Tina down by her arm's off of Pam, her chest and stomach oozed from stab wounds, they turned Pam over her eyes still open, her mouth agape her puss and titties had been sliced like apples. Lewis back was stabbed up. "Well," said Leroy breathlessly. Belinda made a close examination then stood up and shook her head at Leroy. "Damn!" she said coldly. They covered the bodies and headed towards their cars. Belinda grabs another cigarette from out her purse and made a hateful face. "He must die Leroy." she lit the cigarette while inhaling the smoke. The two stood looking over at Cones Mills which was just coming visible with nappy headed black kids running along the dirt paths on each side, the medical examiner boys were coming up the road. "Are you done here Detective?" Cox said from the tracks. "Yeah," Leroy replied back, and then turned to

Belinda. "Do me a favor and ask them noisy ass boys if they saw anything last night," as he motions his eyes over at the bystanders across the rail road tracks. "Sure Leroy, but you know black people don't talk to the police like that."

"Don't believe that bullshit, a nigga will tell on his own mother if he had too, you got to realize there's no loyalty between niggaz."

"Are you leaving?"

"Yup, I've got to go and handle some business, I'll see you later."
Leroy crossed the rail road tracks onto Route 120, the heavy morning traffic had not yet started going into the city but the mall parking lot was almost full. He turned off his radio and made sure his cell phone was on and turned down on 321 to Broadway.

<u>Chapter 39</u>

Leroy drove through Broadway with his brother on his

mind, all he can think about is his desperate plea. *"Get*

me out bro" Leroy drove with the window up while

listening to Power 98 with a quick move he picked up a

DMX CD and inserted in his disc player. He'd been

driving for a couple of hours when he ran a red light.

"Fuck it!" he said to himself. He angrily drove around

Dodge City. Robo nigga the people in the hood called

him, the nigga who has put more muthafucka's behind

bars than Detective Tibbs on *The Heat of the Night,* by

using dirty street tactics and squeezing out dry leads

until they became evidence, Leroy who would do

whatever was necessary to solve a case. Leroy who

they count on to catch the rough neck criminals in the

hood after everyone else was too scared to try. This is

not Leroy Johnson, the one who has failed to solve one of the most important murders in Mecklenburg, the Leroy who can't find the nigga who killed a crack head in Dodge City, the only person who can get his brother out of prison.

Leroy pulled into the ABC store and bought a bottle of Hennessy, he didn't get home until dark. April and Kametica where sitting in the living room watching TV when he walked in from the back door. Leroy tried to hide his fatigue from his daughter as Kametica jumped and wrapped her arms around his neck with Kametica hanging on he kissed her on the cheek. "I'm glad you're home daddy," Kametica said. "Me too sweet cakes, how was your day?"

"Fun, I played kickball at school today." April eyed her.

"I think your daddy would like to relax Kametica, so go upstairs and go to bed you have school in the morning."

Kametica looked around at her mother and pouted. "Girl don't you start that crying because your daddy is here, do you want your ass whup?" April asked. Leroy shot her a dirty look. "No mommy," Kametica replied. "Alright then let's go, you can talk to daddy in the morning," April said. Kametica disappeared. "I wish you wouldn't do that shit," Leroy said. "Do what?" "Talking to her like that, you hurt her feelings."
"I know, but damn Leroy she's spoiled and you're not here half of the time to see that." everything went silent for a moment and April quickly changed the subject. "Well anyway how was your day?" Leroy took a long deep breath and told her about the three dead bodies they found and how he's being played by a nigga that he feels that he can't catch. "Don't worry you'll get him," April said as she tries to comfort him by rubbing him softly on his back. They talked long into the night, planning to sleep late the next morning but the call from

Belinda woke Leroy at eight O'clock, he spoke softly trying not to wake April. "Pam Brown."

"What the hell are you talking about?" Leroy rubbed the cold out of his eyes and looked over at April to make sure that she was still sleep. "Her prints came up in our database."

"What for real?" Leroy bounced up, now on point he remembers her dead body underneath Tina's, he glances over at the clock. "Just chill I'll be right there."

<u>Chapter 40</u>

Leroy drove to the police station, he was tired but the thought of learning the mystery woman identity boost his adrenaline, he parked his car and walked in the building. Leroy greeted Belinda with a smile and a slight pat on the shoulder. "Whatcha got for me." she took in a deep breath and then exhaled. "Well recording to police documents her name is Pam Brown age 35 from Gastonia, been arrested a number of times for possession of crack cocaine, last known address was Holly Hills, here check it out for yourself." Belinda hands him the files and the two walked down the hallway into the break room were Belinda got herself a Mountain Dew and a bag of chips from out of the snack machine and walked over were Leroy was who was sitting at the table still looking over the files. "See anything we can use?" Belinda asked. "Not really!" he paused and then continues. "But these medical jail sheets states that she was receiving pain medication for a tummy tuck that she got days before her arrest." "Tummy tuck, why in the hell would she get something like that for?"

"I don't know but it seems a little odd for a woman of her status."

"Want me to look into it?"

"Nah," Leroy said getting up from the table and handing the documents back to Belinda. "I'll take care of it; just make sure if anybody asks you where I am you tell them you don't know." Belinda gave Leroy a funny look as he was heading towards the break room door. "If you don't mind me asking where are you going?"

"To the place where they do tummy tucks."

"That's in Cleveland County?"

 "Yup, shell town."

"Well you better be careful heard that place is off the chain."

"Don't worry Belinda those niggaz know who to mess with and not to mess with."

"True that," Belinda said as she follows Leroy out the break room.

Leroy knew that the company wouldn't give him the surgeons name over the phone and that it will take a personal trip to the Cleveland County Designer Corp. to squeeze it out of them. The doctor's secondary was very helpful especially after Leroy showed her his badge and photograph of the woman. The lady immediately page the doctor.

"She came here under the name Tabitha Willkie," Dr. Keith Lopez said. Leroy didn't know until the doctor told him but Lopez was quite well known in the Shelby area. He established the Cleveland County Designer Corp for body contouring 12 years prior and was proud of being the first Mexican in North Carolina to advertise chin jobs and tummy tucks on television and radio. "You've seen our commercials haven't you Detective?" as Lopez ran his mouth Leroy seem to remember a commercial showing a white woman at a party thinking about how more beautiful she would look if only she could lose her fat stomach. "That was us," Lopez said with a slight smile. "Now tell me about Mrs. Brown."

"Oh yes, she came to me about three months ago she was dissatisfied with the size of her belly." Lopez took off his glasses and ran his fingers through his salt and pepper hair which contrasted with his light brown colored skin; he tapped the spectacles against the desk and continued. "As we do for all our clients we explained to her the risk and benefits of the procedure, in some cases we ask them to carefully research everything before making a final decision." Leroy didn't care about that but he was curious. "Why is that?" he spoke softly. "Well to tell you the truth a lot of people don't need us as much as they think they do," he went back talking normal. "Hell sometimes I've seen women come in here looking like Halle Barry, body and all." Lopez leaned back in his chair and folded his arms. "I'm not one to turn away business but besides there's no since in telling a client there's nothing wrong with them when only thing they going to do is go somewhere else."

"So you just go along with it like an old hustler and take their money, I like that." Lopez unfolded his arms and leaned forward. "It seems that you like what I do but many people don't, they think it's vain and ungodly but I don't give a shit because I make people feel good about their selves but can they say the same Detective?"

Leroy looked over his shoulder then back at Lopez.

"Tell me more about Ms. Brown."

"I've told you, she came to me because she hated the way her belly looked as I said before I examined her and we discussed the procedure of the operation, my associates and I prepared a computer simulation of what she could expect, she liked what she saw and we performed the surgery."

"Did you suggest she research everything before making a decision?"

"No I did not, it seemed to me that she'd had already made up her mind and knew exactly what she wanted and why she wanted it, to be quite frank she did look a little big in the stomach area."

"How did she pay for the procedure?"

"What do you mean?"

"I mean, did she pay in cash, check or credit card?"

"By check but the then is that the check wasn't written out by her."

"Then who?" Leroy asked with a sense of curiosity.

"His name is Dr. James Spear."

Belinda and other detectives and officers were immediately dispatched to Pam Brown's apartment. The address that Belinda got from police records was an old one and she hadn't yet informed the DMV of the switch. Belinda had to talk to her former landlord who learned from a relative in the neighborhood that she worked as a stripper at a night club in down town Mecklenburg. Where she then went to get her current address. The club unfortunately didn't open until 6 O'clock, around 6:55 the officer radioed headquarters and reported that the apartment was locked and nobody answered his multiple knocks. Belinda ordered him that no one was to enter until her or Leroy got there. KT was coming from the gambling house in Rutherford when he got the call from Belinda to meet her and Leroy at Pam Brown's apartment in Highland. Using a key from the resident manager. Leroy opened the door, standing in the doorway the three stretched their necks to see inside. The place was a little messy but still decent, several sex toys lay scattered on the floor. "You can tell that the woman loved to fuck," said KT as he reached into his case for the camera. While

KT took pictures, Belinda and Leroy moved inside slowly over the carpet floor. Belinda turned to Leroy who was watching KT walk into the bedroom. "This woman was a freak," he said. "There's nothing but sex toys in here." Leroy was about to turn his head towards Belinda when something caught his eye. "Hold up!" he blurted out loud. KT stops in the middle of the bedroom, right foot in midair. "Check this shit out," he pointed about a foot and a half beside Belinda. KT put his right foot down next to his left and walked out of the bedroom. "What did you find?"

 "It looks like a niggaz footprint," replied Leroy. KT took a closer look at the print. "It sure is, there's another one," he said pointing about 16 inches away. "It's more visible can we pick it up?" Leroy asked. "We can try because the pictures aren't going to be good enough there's no contrast," replied KT. He backed up stepping only where he had walked before. "I'll call in the dust print lifter it's not something that I keep in my pocket, tell you the truth I've only used it one time." KT borrowed an officer's radio and contacted one of his people. A voice said it would take about 45 minutes.

"Good-looking," said Leroy. "I bet she was taken from here."

"You think so?"

"Yup and I'll guarantee you someone seen something."

"Unless there was no struggle and no one was paying any attention to what was happening," said Leroy. "You may be right Leroy because I don't see any signs of forced entry," said Belinda. Leroy took out his notebook and wrote the apartment numbers in order, and tore the page in half and handed it to Belinda. "You start from the top and I'll start from the bottom to give us something to do while we wait on KT's homeboy to bring his stuff."

They walked in opposite directions, KT closed the apartment door and went down to his car and read a vibe magazine. About an hour and a half later a blue unmarked car pulled up next to him. The drivers shouted. "Hey KT come and get this shit!" KT looked up. "It's about time nigga I could have gotten that shit myself and stopped along the way for a shot of gin at the bootlegger and gotten here before you."

"Nigga stop fucking whining, they could not find the damn thing. Nobody knew where it was let alone what it was."

"I feel you." KT stepped out of his car and approach Josh, a childhood friend of KTs who voluntarily help him from time to time. "Good looking my nigga," he took the attached case. "You know the state buys shit and doesn't use it."

"That's why these country ass muthafucka's down here are so slow, they don't want to catch up.

So who is it for?"

"Leroy," Josh wanted to be nosy. "Word," he got out of his car and watched as KT place the case on the car hood and checks the contents. Josh had on an XX large T-shirt and a pair of unknown baggy jeans and a wave cap. "Can I watch?" he asked. "I don't care bring your ass on, you might can learn something nigga." Leroy and Belinda were disappointed of the residents they spoke too, because they didn't really know much. Belinda talked to a crack head who said that he didn't see shit because he was too busy smoking dope, but added that he only peeked out the window because he thought someone was coming, and rarely stepped outside except to go get another rock. Leroy spoke to an old white man who had been in bed sick for days and wouldn't have heard anything short of dogs barking walking by his door. The other person he talked to was a young black girl about 18 or 19, said she didn't really want to talk that she had her own problems to deal with. But all of them agreed however that the dead woman was pretty weird and strange and would never talk to nobody. "Make way I'm back," KT said as he and Josh reached the door. "Man I hope you can get me some good looking prints," Leroy said winking at Belinda. "Hey Belinda this is Josh he's the one who brought the stuff and wanted to chill for a second to see how this stuff work… if that's alright with you?" Both Belinda and Leroy nodded as KT opened the apartment door and stepped in cautiously, he got on his hands and knees in front of the first shoe print and opened the attach case next to him, like the guy off of CSI KT worked slowly and desperately. He opened a cardboard mailing tube and removed a thin sheet of plastic, one side was black and the other side was silver, he waved it a few inches above the print and handed it to Josh. "Take the scissors and cut it where my fingers are." he took the cut sheet and put it on the floor next to the print and turned the lights off, he then got down with his face almost to the floor and beamed a flash light over the black side. "You have to make sure there's not a speck of dust." he wiped a few particles away with a rag while Josh turned the lights back on and KT gently placed the sheets black side down over the shoe print, he then took out the high voltage power supply unit, a metal box with several knobs and wires sticking out. There where to large wires connected to it that looked like a TV antenna, KT placed them about an inch away from the sheet, and parallel to it were other wires attached to a thick insulated yellow probe. "Alright Josh plug it up." KT pressed a button and the yellow light on the power supply lit up, he turned the voltage knob to low range and turned to Josh as Leroy and Belinda watched inattentively. "This will produce 5 to 10 kilovolts but don't worry about getting shock because I have this shit down real low." he touched the tip of the high voltage probe at the edge of the sheet, air bubbles in the sheet started to sink into the floor. "It's going a little slower than I thought it would," he said as he turned up the voltage knob. The sheet sank further until finally it was pressed to the floor. KT put a rubble roller over it; he cleared his throat and continued to talk as he rolled. "The electricity goes through the metal antenna and through the floor surface through the sheet and back to the probe, the dust particles are the same charge as the floor and are attracted to the sheet which has an opposite charge, that's why the sheet is attracted to the floor." KT turned off the power supply and waited about 15 seconds and carefully peeled the sheet off the floor, when he flipped it over they saw a complete shoe print down to the cuts and imperfections in the sole and heel. "Turn off the light again Josh," KT asks as he took the sheet and held it at eye level, he motioned for Leroy to run the flash light over it. "A low angle helps you see it better… there you go what do you think Belinda?"

"It's straight." KT unfolded a card board box which had been stored flat in the attachment case. He labeled the sheet, taped it to a thick piece of card board and placed it vertically in the box so nothing touched it. "All right next print," he said.

KT spent the next 30 minutes lifting the second shoe print. "It looks better than the first," said Leroy as he ran the flash light over the sheet. KT gave Leroy a sideways glance. "Do you think that the shoes Joseph found in the truck will match these prints?"

"I don't know but if so then that would mean that our killer has gone from killing men to killing women."

"Alright let's check out what we got?"

KT took measurements of the Air Ones starting with the outside of the shoe calling out the measurements to Leroy who recorded them on a chart sheet. "Next shoe." After taken about seven measurements he turned to the print on the black sheet. "I don't think we can get in-depth measurements but at least we can note some of the obvious high and low points." making sure not to touch the print itself KT held the ruler over the sheet and call out numbers to Leroy who had already drawn a chart called right print, Leroy studied the numbers. "Hey this muthafucka is close… check it out," he said holding the paper so KT could see it. "I be damn," KT said. "Let's do the other shoe." they repeated the process again and held the two charts next to each other. "Bingo!" KT said. Leroy called Belinda on his cell phone. "KT and I measured the shoes with the prints and guess what?" he pauses for a second. "They match, so that means you was right… Pam was taken from her apartment… so I think we should bomb rush the complex tonight."

"I'm down with that."

"Good because we need to check everything inside, her
e-mail, mail box, answer machine and see if we can
narrow it down because I believe that Pam Brown was
the killer's former accomplice. So can you pick me up at
my place around 9 O'clock?"

 "I'll be there."

When they arrived at Brown's apartment building Leroy
jumped out first, he pushed the button for the manager
and was buzzed in. Belinda was right behind and they
looked over the mailbox and found Pam Brown's.
Through the cutout design in the door they could see
letters and magazines jammed together. Leroy reached
into his back pocket and took out a small silver key that
was attached to what look like pink flowers, he looked
at Belinda. "Don't ask." Belinda stood silent watching
Leroy used key that the manager gave him, he opened
the drawer and reached his arm down into Brown's box
and began plucking out mail and handing it to Belinda

when the box was empty he closed it and lock the drawer. They both took the elevator up. "Based on the postmark of the local stuff… I'd say she picked up her mail on Sundays when she didn't have to work," Belinda said. "Anything from you know who?"

"Hell no… just Jet magazines… bills, and junk mail." they peeled off the crime scene tape and entered the immaculate apartment, over by an end table the light was still blinking on the answer machine. They had all agreed that when they examined the room and took the shoe prints to leave the machine along, although it was common thing for homicide detectives to take answer machines from a crime scene. Leroy had discovered recently that the newer models sometimes didn't play back messages properly if the power was cut off, and if the owner didn't rewind the messages once they were listened too, somebody else could mistake it for a recent one instead of a message from last week that had already been played. This was the thing with Browns machine, the message counter said three messages were waiting but after listening to them Leroy also heard four more messages preceding it on the machine. "Where in the hell did you learn this from?" Belinda said. "Been watching them detective shows on TV, from what it sounds like on her recorder... Brown had last listened to her messages on Saturday even... I think it will be alright to ask the neighbors about Sunday and Monday let's bounce."

Leroy went to return the spare key to the building manager, while Belinda headed the opposite direction to knock on apartment doors, 30 minutes later they met up at Belinda's car. "What do you got?"

"Not a damn thing," replied Leroy. "What about you?"

"Well." Belinda opened up her notepad. "I talked to a man who lives in the back who said he was looking out his window when he saw a man dressed in a FedEx uniform pulling up in a federal express truck beside the apartment trash cans and parked and ran inside the building. He didn't see him come out but when he looked out the window about an hour and a half later the truck was gone."

"Did he describe the guy?"

"Yeah, black and in his late 30s or early 40s."

"Belinda, I'm not trying to sound like one of them NAACP niggaz but how many black people do you know works for the federal express in this red neck ass city?"

"None," said Belinda. "Is there any way to check with the company about whether they still practice the Jim Crow laws?" Leroy shot Belinda a look and they both laughed. "Well, do you think it was him?" Belinda asked. "You damn right I think it was him, this nigga is a perfectionist; he's going to do whatever he can not to get caught even if it means putting on different faces.

Like the time him and his lady friend played the hell out

of me and Cox at the station." then all of a sudden

without warning Leroy exploded. "Dammit!" he shouted

in frustration hitting his fist on the dash board in

Belinda's car. "What in the hell is wrong with you

Leroy?" Belinda asked. Leroy took in a deep breath and

then exhale. "Well," he paused for a second and then

continued. "I forgot to tell you what all happened the

night when we released Lewis Brooks."

"Oh the Capt. told me..."

"Just shut up and let me talk," Leroy said cutting her off.

"The killer was at the station---him and some white

bitch… the nigga claim to be Brooks coo, coo doctor

but I knew something was up just by the way he looked.

I knew he was disguised so I just figure that he was

working for the killer, so I played along hoping that the

three would lead me to him but I was wrong, the

muthafucka was right in my face playing me like a damn sucker."

"So you know who he is?"

"No, not exactly but I know he goes by the name Dr. James Spear."

"You think so?"

"I know so because it all adds up now, from what my momma told me about the letters to what the Dr. told me in Shelby I think the nigga got alias." Belinda eased the car in front of Leroy's crib. "Want to come in and chill for a minute? April is at work."

"Nah, that's alright," Belinda said. "Why not… are you going to some other man's crib?"

"Yup but it's not a guy it's a lady friend of mine."

"Is she pretty or ugly?"

 "I guess she's pretty why?"

"Because if she's fine I like to meet her," Leroy said getting out the car. "Perhaps I might if you stop trying to hit on me." Leroy didn't respond. "I guess that's a no."

she didn't respond back so he closed the car door and

walked towards the front porch picking up the

newspaper along the way. Belinda pecked the horn

twice as she waves to him bye and peels out.

Chapter 41

Belinda parked her car in downtown Mecklenburg and

walked up and down the strip looking for Halley.

 She made a few stops but hadn't spotted her in all the

dangerous places; she glanced inside Drop-in cupping

her face against a dirty plate glass window, sometimes

she'd talk with the night clerk, a Nigerian college

student who gave Halley money in exchange for a blow

job but hadn't seen her since then.

Ever since her husband left her Belinda has been

finding comfort from a lot of men but none had Halley's

warmth, a gentleness that went through her, a love that

seem real even though Belinda knew it wasn't. She had reminded herself many times before that Halley was a trick who would fuck whom ever came up with the most paper but still she was jealous of her fucking other men. Deep down she had feelings for her, she knew she was being stupid feeling this way about her but she couldn't help herself, she desired a woman's touch even if she had to pay for it. Belinda had been with a woman before but just never been with one quiet like Halley, maybe because she never had to pay for it, no commitments, no strings attached, having a relationship with a prostitute never crossed her mind. Belinda wanted desperately to talk to Halley about their last meeting at the Holiday Inn, the only time she really wanted her to spend the night with her. "*What was up with that, was she trying to take their relationship to another level?*" her pussy got wet every time she thought about that night. As Belinda looked up the street, she thinks she sees Halley; she couldn't call to her, too far up the road. The people around would hear, she ran quickly up the street in her direction, she saw her thick body make a sharp turn on to the side walk. It was Halley, she knew it was her, she shouted, did the bitch turn around to see who was calling her? *"Hell no!"* Belinda ran after her. Her heart beating fast as hell. *"Halley!"* she called out again under her breath. Just as she got closer she noticed Halley speaking to a man in a blue car and vanished inside the vehicle. Belinda watches the car pull away. The man driving was wearing a red and green Rasta Crown with shades. As they drove up on 3rd St., Belinda could see Halley lean over towards the driver and disappear. Belinda closed her eyes, took a deep breath and took her foot and kicked the side of the building wall, she thought what the point of pitching a fit but she did anyway.

Leroy was sitting at his desk on the phone talking to a private business associate of his when Belinda walked in with an exhaustive look on her face, her eyes red and a little swollen, cutting his conversation short Leroy quickly hung up the phone. "Hey Belinda, what's up?" Leroy said getting up from his desk. Belinda ignored him and went into her office, Leroy followed. "Are you alright Belinda?"

"Yeah, I'm just tired as hell." Leroy began to say something when suddenly Cox stuck his head in the door. "Detective, I need to see you in my office immediately," Cox said with a serious look on his face. Leroy nodded his head at Cox and then turned his attention back to Belinda. "I'll be right back Belinda." Minutes later Leroy was in Cox office. "Shut the door," Cox said hatefully. The room turned suddenly very quiet, even the noise from outside the office didn't intrude; Leroy sat down in the chair. "What's on your mind this time Capt.?" he tried to sound calm and collective. Cox didn't respond, he just stood there motionless in front of his desk with a small yellow envelope in his hand. "Come on man talk to me what's on your mind?" Leroy said again this time with a little concern in his voice. "Can you explain this Detective?" Cox tossed the envelope in Leroy's lap and then sat down; he reached inside the yellow package and took out several photos. "What the hell is this?" Leroy asked. "You tell me?" Cox said. Leroy glanced through the pictures and then slung them on Cox desk. "This is bullshit… it's not what you think," he pauses for a second and then added. "I was undercover." Cox slowly leaned up in his chair pulling a photo from out of the package. "Is that right?" Cox said with a smirk on his face. "Then explain to me why are you seen here in this picture performing what appears to be illegal activity?" Leroy suddenly shifts his head away from Cox. "Look at me!" Cox shouted holding up the picture. "Here you are with some unidentified nigga exchanging what appears to be weapons and cocaine."

"That shit doesn't prove anything," Leroy said. "Oh no, what about this one?" Cox held up another photo in Leroy's face. "Here you are again… this time with a prostitute who have visited our jail number of times… if I can remember her name I think was Halley King. Here's the two of you checking into the Super 8 Motel, want me to keep going Detective? Or should I say ex detective because I have enough evidence right here to nail your black ass to the wall," Cox said. Right then Leroy immediately realized his career was over, all he could do now was just sit there and look crazy, shaking his head thinking if he should make a run for it, call April and tell her to pack her and Kametica things and meet him at the airport.

"Okay Capt., you got me so now what is you going to do, turn me in?" Leroy asked. Cox slowly leaned back in his chair with a slight smile on his face. "For all it's worth just to watch you suffer Johnson, I'm going to keep this matter on the low, besides I don't want to be seen as another black man, bringing another black man down… if you know what I mean. So what I'm going to do since I don't know who sent me these photos, I'm going to let it slide for right now but whoever it was sure can't stand your ass." Leroy started to say something when Cox motions him not to speak. "I decided to keep you on the job for the moment just until this so-called Bible killer is caught." Cox stood up from his chair and started gathering up his things from off his desk and then add. "I also want you to turn in your badge when this is all over is that understood?"

"Yeah… is that all?" Leroy asked as he started to get up from his chair. "And one more thing," Cox said calmly. "I also want your black ass out of Mecklenburg… I don't think I can live with myself knowing that someone like you is still roaming around in my district."

Chapter 42

In the auto shop parking lot Leroy met Nah-G, the man who been pushing crack from out of his shop for years. Despite coming unexpectedly Leroy didn't bother in explaining why he popped up without warning. "What's up my nigga?" as the two embraced each other Leroy immediately motioned Nah-G to get in his car so that he wouldn't be seen out in the open.

Leroy knew Nah-G when they were in high school, one time they came across a Mexican drug dealer who supplied members of the Governor's inner circle with high grade cocaine, one day without warning the two found themselves being interrogated by a FBI agent, they were so shocked at the lack of evidence they couldn't help themselves from laughing at every word that came out of the agent mouth that could have been why Leroy found Nah-G as a hell of a crime partner, they were too much alike. Nah-G wore steel toe boots with an auto shirt uniform with a name tag attached to his chest, he took a seat in the passenger side of Leroy's Crown Vick. "What is this all about? If it's about your cut I…"

"I'm not here for that," Leroy said cutting him off. "I'm here to tell you we both going to have to chill for a while," Leroy pauses and then adds. "I mean just for right now."

"What the hell are you talking about?" Nah-G asked with a very concerned look on his face. "What I'm saying is if we don't chill out we're going to be behind bars."

"Damn… you mean they're on to us?"

"Well not really," Leroy said as he rubs his hand across his face and then continues. "But they will soon if I don't figure us a way out of this mess."

"Then what's your plan?" Leroy didn't respond but did give Nah-G an uneasy look. "Well, what are we going to do?" Leroy reached into the backseat and grabbed a white envelope and handed it to Nah-G. "What the hell you want me to do with this?"

 "I need you to give it to Smoke."

"Smoke!" Nah-G snapped back. "You mean Hitman Smoke?"

"Yeah, I've already spoke to him yesterday about what I need him to do."

"Don't tell me you need him to kill somebody?" Nah-G ask jokingly. "That's exactly what I need him to do," Leroy said coldly. "Are you serious?"

"I don't have any other choice alright!" Leroy said raising his voice a little. "Now you just tell him there is $20,000 dollars and a full description of the target in that envelope as he requested." Nah-G stuck the envelope in his back pocket and started to get out of the car when he suddenly turned his attention back to Leroy. "What do you want me to do in the meantime?"

"Just lay low and I'll let you know when things are back to normal, you just make sure you give that to Smoke," Leroy said pointing his finger at Nah-G.

Nah-G nodded his head. "Alright if this shit blows up in your face you just make sure you don't put my name in it," Nah- G said as he hops out of the car. Without responding Leroy put the car in reverse and peels out of the parking lot.

<u>Chapter 43</u>

James put his hands around her ass and pulled her close, they kissed and Eve arched her neck back and then touched a finger to his lips. "I would really love to see Capt. Cox face when he sees them photos… do you?"

"Oh yes, especially Detective Johnsons the man who everyone expects to catch me," James said as he takes his hands off her and makes his way to the fridge to grab a beer. "I would like to see his face when they throw his ass in prison with his brother," he added. "Me too, it's like you said neither of them suspect anything about us. It's as if everything you said will happen is now falling in place isn't it?" James thought for a minute before answering. "So far it's been going the way I've planned but there's still something missing… it lacks that final ending… a… standing ovation."

"Oh James, I like when you talk with so much wisdom." They both smile as James placed his beer on the coffee table and flopped on the couch. Eve followed him and collapsed her legs underneath her body on the floor in front of him, her robe was opened exposing her white breast, she handing him his beer from off the table and placed her head in between his legs. He stroked her hair.

"James," she said staring up at him. "Do you think he knows what you're about?"

"Nobody knows what I've been through… what I've endured… what I've lost," his voice had an edge. She picked her head up, looked in his eyes. "Oh James," she said in a kid's voice. "I still haven't got my get back from yesterday." James started to say something when suddenly Eve bolted up right and bounced like a rabbit. He tried to protect himself by crossing his hands in front of his face but they flared out when she pitch him, the can of beer went flying. "Yell!" she shouted. "Gotcha!"

"You bitch."

"I gotcha, I gotcha," she continued pitching him until he demanded her to stop. Finally they nestled together on the couch. She pulled off his shirt, played with his nappy chest hairs. "Do you think he enjoyed our video?" she asked. "I suspect he's seen it a 1000 times, probably jacking off on it. Who knows he might just figure it all out," his voice became sincere. "We were kidding about it before but this is serious." he held her face in his hands. "Nobody will figure it out Eve, no one." she buried her face on his shoulder. "If you say

so," she whispered.

<u>Chapter 44</u>

The number that appeared on Leroy cell phone was his

mother but he couldn't answer it right then, he was too

busy going over old notes and clues that was left by the

killer. When he was done he sat in deep thought, the

vibrator on his cell phone wobble again. The same

number, Leroy finally answered. "It's about time you

pick up the damn phone."

"Mom I thought you were out of town, why aren't you

not at the bike fest flirting with them young guys… what

Todd got you on lock down?"

"No listen son I've got something very important to talk to you about so come by the house, I've also have something to show you."

"C'mon mom I don't have any time for games."

"Stop talking and just bring your tail out here, you're going to want to see this."

"What is it about?" the phone went dead. "*That woman is crazy,*" Leroy whispered to himself and headed out the precinct. Leroy's mom lived in a pretty good neighborhood called Little Africa, a vibrant mill town from the turn of the century until the 1930s when it was incorporated by the city of Watts, losing its original name of Lillington with industrial mills all but gone over sea's, developers were thinking about turning the massive unused land into a continuation of Mecklenburg along Broadway. The seven foot fence that surrounded the area kept outsiders from coming in, especially dope dealers who could no longer hustle in their hood and were searching for a safer place to set up shop. Already illegal immigrants from Cleveland County were descending upon Little Africa on hard working class blacks causing the property value to drop. Like other black folks in Little Africa, Marie wanted them wet backs to stay out. Marie's house had been built for an Irish family in the early 1900s and had an upstairs and a downstairs with four separate bed rooms, three on the top floor one on the bottom with a large living room, two baths and a basement. The porch was rebuilt a year ago with pine wood and was surrounded by plotted plants; her garden was covered with vegetables. Leroy always thought that his moms crib reminded him of one of them plantation houses on Mississippi burning. Inside the place was neat and cozy but still smelt like pig's feet.

Marie Johnson answered the door wearing a dark blue night gown and bed room slippers. "Boy what took you so long?" she said waving a glass of ice tea in Leroy's face. She walked to the kitchen placing the cup in the sink and opens the fridge. "Hungry?"

"Nah," Leroy said. "Come in here," Marie commanded. Leroy followed her out of the kitchen and into the living room, immediately Leroy noticed a stack of books on the coffee table. "Is this what you call me down here for to show me a bunch of books?"

"Stop being so close minded and come over here and take a seat," she said patting her hand on the couch suggesting for him to sit next to her. "What is this all about anyway?" Leroy asked as he flops on the sofa. Without responding Marie hands him a white and gold book with the name title, (English writers) looking over it he started to say something when Marie cut him off. "Open the book and turn to page 72 and read the top sentence." with a curious look on his face he opened it up to the page and began to read.

"The people of the Church of England gather around and ask him. (Oh Shakespeare we know you are a man of much wisdom and gifts but who in the name of God order you to tamper with the words of the Almighty) and Shakespeare replied saying. "It was our king who ordered me to revise the Bible in our native tongue so that all of England can understand"

With a strange look on his face Leroy closed the book and handed it back to his mother. "What is all this supposed to mean?" Marie laid the book on the table and looked over at her son. "Boy is you slow?" she said sharply. "What it means is that the Bible killer's full name is James Shakespeare." in shock Leroy stood up from the couch. "It can't be."

"I thought the same thing until when I discovered that the name Shakespeare is what the killer was talking about when he said he wanted me to write my name and age in it, meaning the Bible." the room went silent for a second. "Oh you don't believe me take a look for yourself." Marie leaned over and snatched her black King James Bible from off the lab stand and handed it to Leroy. "It's in psalms chapter 46 versus 3 and 9 is where you will find his name and age." turning to it he reads....

(Though the mountains 'shake' with its swelling, he breaks the bow and cuts the 'spear' in two.)

 After reading it he tossed the black book on the sofa and walked across the room, turning his back to his mother he finally spoke. "It's hard for me to believe a man like that who has been a preacher for over eight years would all of a sudden flip like that."

"Believe it," Marie shot back.

"But why would he kill?"

 "Revenge son, revenge or have you forgotten that James Shakespeare is Amy Shakespeare's husband."

"Oh shit," Leroy blurted out with one hand on his head. "I should have known... that will explain why my name is in the notes... he wants to destroy me for what he thinks my brother done to his wife, and I have to stop him." Leroy started towards the door when Marie suddenly stood up. "Wait you can't just go after this guy."

"Why can't I?"

"Because what you have is just circumstantial evidences and not facts son."

"So what do you want me to do? Wait for him to make his next move."

"That wouldn't be a bad idea, given the fact that he's planned something big."

"What do you mean?" without responding Marie reached into her back pocket and took out a small note and handed it to Leroy. "What is this?"

"It's from the killer, I meant to tell you when you got here but it slipped my mind." Leroy opened the note and read it silently to himself.

"Roses are red, violets are blue, just because you're career is through doesn't mean you have to give up so soon, because after this last kill you going to wish I killed you."

A.k.a. Bible killer

"Where did you get this note from?"

"April said it came in the mail yesterday and that you being so busy she felt it was best not to worry you with it, so she brought it to me to try to make sense of it."

 "What the hell was she thinking?" Leroy mutters to himself. "Mom I need you to stay here and lock the doors."

"Why?"

"Because I have a feeling whoever he's planned on killing is someone close to me."

Chapter 45

For the first time in his life Leroy felt a sense of fear, not only for his family but for himself as well, there were still a lot of unanswered questions but it didn't matter because if his mother was right and Shakespeare is the killer, who's main objective is to take his revenge out on him. Then he needed to find this nigga before he tries to take a shot at one of his own.

Belinda was working in her office when her cell phone rang. "Yes, this is Lieut. Bright can I help you?"

"Belinda it's me."

"Leroy where are you?"

"I've been trying too ---"

"No time to talk --- I just need you to meet me at the station."

"But why do…"

"I will explain everything when I get there." the phone immediately went dead.

Leroy hadn't spoken to Cox since there occasion in his office yesterday, as usual they were ignoring each other. "You got to be fucking kidding me," Belinda said as her and Leroy walked towards the Capt.'s office. "So you mean to tell me that James Shakespeare the preacher is our man?"

"Yup but he's not a preacher anymore, word has it that he left town right after my brother's trial and never came back."

"Yeah, everything but the never came back part," Belinda said with a shitty smile.

Cox was on the phone, and he stared up and said. "I'll be looking forward to it Sir... talk to you later... bye." he took some time straighten up his desk and said with a grin on his face. "Just who I wanted to see my favorite sidekicks, have a seat." Belinda and Leroy sat at attention with puzzled looks on their faces. "That was the head man in charge, said he got a letter today from our boy and all it said was get ready for my big kill because it's about to go down. They're sending it here now, it contained a police badge."

"*I was right,*" Leroy said under his breath. "What you say?" Belinda asked over hearing Leroy saying something. "Oh I just remember to tell you that I received a letter from the killer stating that he was planning something big, like taking out somebody close to me maybe someone I love dearly."

"Dammit Leroy you didn't tell me that part."

"I didn't feel it was necessary, besides I don't need you going all Wonder Woman on me and stuff."

"What's that supposed to mean?"

"Nothing," said Leroy shaking his head. "In case you don't know, were in this shit together Leroy. So if you in some type of danger I want to know about it, I shouldn't have to hear it from you at the last minute."

"Just shut up both of you," Cox interrupted who only caught the end of the conversation. "The way I see it the two of you have not done jack shit to catch this guy, so I have decided to take you two clowns off the case."

"You can't do that."

"Oh no watch me. You're off the case turn over all your notes to Detective Jasmine."

"You know what Cox---I used to think you were real but I was wrong… you are a fake… you need me and you know it."

"Is that right, prove it? Show me what you got… give me one good reason why I should keep you on this case?"

"The killer is James Shakespeare," Leroy said. "Yeah right, and I'm Bill Gates."

"He's telling the truth Captain," Belinda blurted out. "I know all of this sounds hard for you to believe but your ex-pastor has been behind this mess from the very beginning."

"You damn right it's hard for me to believe but then again you may be right… the man did hate you Johnson," Cox said cutting his eyes over at Leroy. Leroy ignored the slick comment and explained to him what was going on. "Do you know how stupid that shit sounds?" Cox said. "Besides if you are right there's not enough evidence to make an arrest anyway, everything you have is circumstantial."

"That may be but he might be planning to kill again, and if so I'm going to be there waiting."

"Same here," said Belinda. Cox thought for a moment. "Belinda are you really sure about this?"

"It's the best lead we got."

"Three days that's all… I'll tell the Chief… I don't want y'all coming to me begging for another chance if this crap fails." the two started to get up when Cox added. "Another thing Leroy… I'm not doing this because I trust you… I'm doing this because I trust the white girl. I don't think she would risk her job on something foolish would you?" Cox turned his attention from Leroy and held a mean glare at Belinda and smile. Belinda squint her eyes at Cox. "Oh yeah before I go Captain, I need you to do something for me," Leroy said. "What's that?" Cox said gritting his teeth. "I need you to send someone to patrol my mother's house full time."

"Done--- anything else?" Leroy started to say something when Cox cut him off. "Never mind get the fuck out."

"Oh that's how it is?" Cox tensed his body then settle back into his chair. "For you it is." he leaned forward. "Or have you forgotten our little discussion yesterday, if not then you should know there's nothing else for us to talk about."

"This isn't over Captain." Cox responded by smiling widely while Leroy and Belinda got up and headed out the door. When they were clear from the office Belinda turned to Leroy. "What the hell was that all about?"

"Oh nothing Belinda, nothing I can't handle."

Chapter 46

Eve pulled her white Lincoln into the parking lot at William & Hart and walked inside the building and stood in the waiting room. She wasn't sure if she came through the right entrance, wearing a blue narrow stripe navy pencil skirt and blue high heels. She looked at her watch and glanced around furtively. *"This can't be right there's no one here,"* she said to herself and walked outside towards the back of the main building. The area was empty for a Friday afternoon, business men were getting in their fancy cars and going home for the weekend. The security guard inside the facility eye balled her as she stepped through the metal detector and down the hallway with a smile she knew exactly what the guard was looking at.

At Mecklenburg Elementary, a bunch of kids were playing dodge ball, in the middle was Jay Logan. They deliberately wouldn't stop hitting him with the ball, whose large round belly jiggle when he moved. As the boys and girls continued hitting him with the ball around the school playground, jumping and laughing he tried to catch it but his spastic movements only made them torment him even more to where he just ran off the playground and cried. Then suddenly the playing stopped as a tall black man stepped out of the school building and approach the small students. The crowd broke when the man pointed to the kid holding the ball and screamed for him to go and apologize. The boy responded immediately and walked sheepishly towards the pouting kid. "Hey you," the man said to another kid on the monkey bars. "Help him with his stuff."

"But I didn't do anything," the kid said. "What did I say? Do it boy!" the man waited patiently as the boy tried to help Jay with his things but he wouldn't let him. "Go away I don't need your help punk." he put his jacket over his shoulder, found his lunchbox and walked inside the building trying to play as if nothing happen. The hateful man looked around and pointed. "I want you to go to the principal's office."

"But I…."

"Go right now girl." the girl looked around scared. "I think he's new here because I've never seen him before," one kid said. "Y'all shut up!" the man shouted as he watched the little girl walked towards the building. "Hey wait a second, don't I know you?"

"No sir I don't think so."

"Yeah I do… you're April and Leroy's little girl aren't you?" Kametica stood frozen. "Your daddy is a police man isn't he?" no response. "He wants' me to take you to your mother's house immediately, doesn't she work for William & Hart?"

"Yeah," the little girl replied. The man looked around at the rest of the kids. "Now y'all knuckle heads go inside and be grateful that I didn't take my belt off - now go! Let's go little lady we don't want your mother waiting."

The front lobby of William & Hart was deck out with posters of the company's home base of Texas with its nicely paneled walls and marble floors. The office behind the front desk was divided into cubits, each having its own computer and fax machine, newspaper clippings were thumb tacked to the outside of each one.

"Is Scott Gates in today?" the woman said to April Carson. "He told me to meet him here, we've got tickets to the Hornets game tonight."

"Alright give me a minute and I'll page him for you," April replied. "Who are the Hornets playing against?" the woman didn't have time to respond when April signal her finger for her to hold that thought while she answers the phone, her face showed fear. "What? Oh my God where? When? I'm on my way."

"What happened asked the woman?"

"My baby Kametica she's…I have to go get her."

 "Let me take you I have a car."

"Alright let's go." as the two hustled outside the woman pointed to her Lincoln that was parked around front. April thought it was a little strange that this white lady knew she didn't have a car but she didn't dwell on it for more than a second before she passed out. The last thing she remembered was feeling a hard object hitting her in the back of her head.

The secretary put her Vibe magazine down on the desk and glanced out the window, when suddenly the phone rang. "Hello this is Mary Green Homicide can I help you?"

"Tell Johnson to bring his ass out to the parking lot bitch!" without hesitating she immediately slam the phone and buzzed Leroy on the intercom. He and Belinda were discussing their next move when he receive the call, as the two made it to the front desk Leroy noticed an angry look on Mary face. "What's up Mary is something wrong?"

"I just got a call a minute ago, telling me to tell you to go out to the parking lot."

"Who was it?"

"Don't know, didn't ask. I just slam the phone and immediately page you." Leroy looked at Belinda who was waiting for him to respond. "Maybe it's our guy."

"Well let's go see." as the two headed out Mary called out to them. "Make sure you whup his ass for calling me a bitch," she said as she went back reading her magazine. "What the hell is that?" Belinda asked as she squint her eyes trying to make out the object that was lying on the ground. Leroy stood paralyzed. "It's my daughter's book bag and April's purse - that nigga has my family Belinda... he has my family."

Leroy picked up the book bag and purse and held it in his hand, and rushed to his car. "Leroy wait!" Belinda shouted. "Where are you going?"

"I'm going to find them dammit!" Leroy said almost out of breath. "I'm coming with you."

"No! You stay here just in case he calls back." Leroy tried to put his thoughts together, he had been going plum crazy driving around the city since talking to Kametica's teachers at the school and learning about April's disappearance from William & Hart. *"Did he get KT too?"* he thought.

An hour later he burst into Cox office. Cox looked shocked. "The nigga has my daughter and April and probably KT," Leroy said. "I know Belinda told me and KT is alright I just spoke to him a minute ago but never mind that, what is this about you receiving a letter from the killer?" Leroy explained. Cox picked up the phone and looked at Leroy solidly. "Leroy listen man --- even though we have been going through our drama I wouldn't wish this shit on no one you feel me?" Cox passes the phone to Leroy, it was KT on the other end. "Hey man he's got Kametica and April."

"What wait - who?"

"The killer is James."

"Wait… slow the hell down --- James who?"

"James Shakespeare he's the damn killer."

"How you know?" Leroy broke down the whole story to KT, while Cox called communications from his other phone, he demanded the dispatcher to have every detective not working a crime scene to report to headquarters immediately. Cox looked at Leroy. "I'll let them know what's up when they call in --- give me a description on what they were wearing. Don't worry Leroy we'll find them." Leroy punches the wall with his fist. "FUCK!" he was frustrated not knowing what to do next, he had to think. Finally calls from detectives came in and Cox quickly orders a team to the school and another to William & Hart. "That would do it," said Cox. "Have you spoken to Belinda since you been back?"

"No why?"

"Told me she had to go to the emergency room --- said a friend of hers was badly beaten and…"

Before Cox could finish Leroy immediately rushed out the door. "Leroy wait!" the secondary shouted. "Sgt. Lincoln called and left a message saying to tell you that he couldn't find anything on your guy either… he said it's like the name doesn't exist."

"She called for you Lieut. That's why we contact you first."

 "How is she doing?"

"Not too good, I'm sorry," he touched her shoulder and looked into her eyes. "Hurry, she doesn't have that much time left." Belinda kneeled beside the bed as the nurse pulled the curtain around them, Halley turned her head. Belinda didn't say anything to her immediately.

She waited silently until she did. "Belinda I need you to… stop him," her mouth strained to move, and her eyes was swollen shut. "Who are you talking about - stop who?" she coughed and took a deep breath. Belinda rub her hair softly pushing her hair off her face. "Halley you need to tell me who done this?"

"It was Detect…" she coughed again. "LJ… he was my pimp… he thought I had something to… do with."

"Do with what --- who's LJ Halley?" closer, Belinda put her ear to her mouth and she felt puffs of her breath as she tried to say something to her. Seconds later without warning she gasped and coughed multiple times, the ECG machine emitted a buzz, within moment's three nurses and a doctor ripped open the curtain and pushed Belinda out of the way almost knocking her down. "Please get out!" one of them said as they crowd over her body. Belinda heard the doctor giving orders as she walked away. In the lobby she got herself a coke and a bag of Doritos and lean up against the drink machine thinking about what Halley was trying to tell her. The doctor approached her 30 minutes later. "I'm very sorry we did all we could do, are you a family member?" she hesitated. Oh... um... no! Well I am in a way she has no other family." the doctor scratched his head and cleared his throat. "Okay well I'm going to need you to see that young lady over there behind the desk and fill out some forms." he pointed to a semicircular desk in the middle of the hall. "Just show her you're ID and tell her what it's for and she will hook you right up, and again I'm very sorry for your loss." with that he walked away. Belinda placed her hands on the counter and when the woman acknowledged her presence she said. "Yes, I'm here on the behalf of Halley King I understand there's forms that I need to fill out."

Chapter 47

The basement was dark, the cold cement floor felt sticky and nasty as she picked herself off the floor. The back of her head felt sore, she immediately noticed blood on her fingers after she touched it, in shock she staggered backwards, her head spinning. Her balance still off, she couldn't see anything in the basement to hold on too. She didn't remember coming here, so how did she get here she thought. She tried to walk forward but took three steps and collapsed in a heap of trash, her memory returned in pictures. *"Oh my God my little girl is in danger…white lady in a white Lincoln,"* she shook her head and her eyes began to adjust and the walls around her became a little clearer. *"My baby, where is she?"* shaking it off again April made it to her feet and reached for the wall, she concentrated on each step patting the walls with her palms. *"How do I get out of here?"* she said to herself. She spun around and notice a set of stairs that lead to a small door, her vision was still dark and blurry. April squinted trying to focus, staggering she lurched for the steps gripping each one like a mountain lion as she slowly climbs her way to the top. Suddenly the door swung open and she was being pushed back down the steps. She tried to get up but couldn't keep her balance. She tried to stop herself from moving by clinching on the arm rail but each time she tried the person holding her pushed harder, then all of a sudden the pushing stop, she was exhausted, her body on the floor breathing hard nobody entered. She got up and stares at the door, all she could hear were the sounds of footsteps moving away.

"He's took Kametica and April," Leroy said solemnly. Marie put down her remote and looked at Leroy. "Oh Lord when… how?"

"It was sometime this morning I was told he was at the school claiming to be a good friend of mine and that I wanted him to pick up Kametica, a lady at the school found it a little suspicious and called April at work but about that time it was too late."

"What about April?" Marie said nervously. "It was said that she was last seen leaving out with a white lady, my guess it's the same white girl I met at the station claiming to be Lewis's lawyer." Marie flinches and stood up to face Leroy. "I promise you if anything happens to my…"

"Don't worry mom, we already have the city surrounded." with that the phone rang and Leroy grabbed it. "Hello?"

"It's Capt. Cox. I thought you would be there."

"What's up Captain?"

"Good news we may have a location on your boy whereabouts." Leroy's body tensed. "Where?"

"I can't say until we know for sure."

"Dammit Cox!" Leroy paused. I'm on my way there." he felt the sweat dripping down his face as he put the phone down slowly. "What did he say any word on my granddaughter and April?" Marie asked in patiently. "No mom, just stay here and I'll call you if anything comes up." he quickly kissed his mom on the cheek and immediately headed out the door.

 Feeling her way back up the steps April headed towards the door again, squinting she saw a light coming from out the keyhole beneath the door knob. She grabs the knob and waited, on the other side a child was crying. April twisted and tug on the knob desperately until the unstable door rip open.

"*Kametica!*" the little girl was tied down to a chair, her mouth cover with duct tape, her cloths and hair was dirty, Kametica's eyes got big and began wiggling wildly when she looked at her mother in fear. "It's going to be okay honey," April said as she held her tiny face in her hands. Slowly she pulled the tape from her lips. "Oh God baby is you alright?" no response, April notice Kametica watery brown eyes staring past her. "Of course she's alright," the voice behind her said. "But not for long." April quickly turned. "Don't worry I'm going to make it as painless as possible."

"Pastor Shakespeare." frozen in disbelief April had trouble getting her words together. "But you are a…"

"What?" a man of God, I'm sorry sister but my days of being a Jesus freak is over, it's time for me to do what God don't have the guts to do." April stood up between James and Kametica hiding her daughter from the man's view. "I tried to be a God fearing man but what did I get in return --- not shit so I decided to take the law in my own hands, punish those who I felt was responsible for my lost."

"What in the hell is you talking about?" April asked curiously. "Come on now," he said with a smirk on his face. "Woman you know exactly what I'm talking about, the dope dealers the gang bangers, the filth that keeps our neighborhoods polluted. They are the problem." he pause for a short second as April kept side stepping keeping herself between him and Kametica as James walked slowly around the room. He stopped and stared at a picture of himself on the wall. It was the first time April actually noticed her surroundings, she was distasteful by the way the room look with beer cans and candy wrappers all over the floor, four small bookcases stuff with bibles hung on the wall, a large leather sofa with roaches crawling in an out of it fit snugly in the corner. "Do you understand now April?" he said calmly. "This shit isn't about you personally, it's about your baby daddy who thinks he can flood the ghetto with crack, and at the same time play the hero."

"What are you saying? That's insane."

"Oh you must don't remember my precious Amy who was practically murdered by Leroy brother Tyrone Johnson --- he tried to defend him knowing damn well he was guilty as hell."

 "But he was found guilty," April shot back. With a low giggle he began putting on latex gloves and glanced at April. "Oh you still don't get it do you? I'm not doing this because of what Tyrone did, I'm doing this because of what Leroy did." April looked at him awkward but kept quiet. "The police report stated that Amy was poison by Tyrone who I think was just another pawn in Leroy's little sick game. It was him who had her killed not Tyrone --- he was just carrying out orders."

"What?" April said confusedly. "Yeah that's right… it was Leroy who gave Tyrone that bad dope to give Amy."

"That's ridiculous --- why would he do that?"

"Because he was her damn pimp, she wanted out so he took her out."

"I didn't mean to…"

 "Didn't mean to do what? Get me upset --- oh no April I have no beef against you. You have to believe me… it's just that Leroy has to pay for what he's done to me and to the people he's use. You can understand that can you?"

"Why murder?" April asked as she kept her eyes glued to James, her hands behind her gripping Kametica's arm's which were still tied down to the chair. "Oh those niggaz were just trophies of my, they didn't whole no real significance to my plan. Not only that they needed

to die --- no one wants lowlifes like that in their

neighborhoods, people should be thanking me not

criticizing me."

"Then why not let her go she hasn't done anything,

she's not any drug dealer or gang member she's just a

baby." April said referring to her daughter who sat

quietly as the two continued to conversant. "I can't do

that because I need Johnson to know how it feels to

lose some one he loves." James said stomping around

the room like a mad man. When he finally stopped he

retrieve a gold bible from out of the small bookcase. "Sit

the fuck down." April didn't move. "Now!" he shouted.

"Don't let me have to tell you again," he slung the book

at her. "Here read this and pray that I just kill you and

spare your lovely daughter." with that being said he

glanced over at Kametica with a shitty smile and

headed for the door. "I'll be back, so don't try anything

sneaky." once the door was shut April kneeled down in front of Kametica. "Honey is you alright? Say something." Kametica didn't respond she was still terrified, all she could do was whine, April tried to untie the tiny rope but couldn't, she tried to bite it loose with her teeth but it was no use. She ran to the door and pull, it was lock from the outside. April looked back at Kametica and then down at the floor where the book landed, the front cover was open and she saw pictures and hand written notes scattered around it. She bent down on her knees and picked up one of the notes and opened it and read the first three sentences, the letter seem to been written over 10 years ago. "*She was going to turn him in,"* she whispered to herself. The letter was old and fragile and as she continued reading she became more shock with each word. She looked up at Kametica who was shivering and then back at the note, her hands began to shake so much she could barely finish reading. When she was done she sat in the floor motionless, she looked again at Kametica and went to her, kneeling she put her head in the girls lap. James Shakespeare watched the scene from his surveys camera in the other room and smiled.

Chapter 48

Leroy and KT met in the front lobby; KT was responding to a call from Cox to report to his office. "Are you doing alright man?"

"Yeah man I'm doing alright," Leroy said after the two embraced each other. "Nigga you been drinking?"

"Hell nah man." Leroy sniffed KT up and down. "Yes the fuck you have… you need to take your ass home."

"Man I want this guy as bad as you do, so don't try to cut me out." Leroy started to ignore him but responded anyway. "Look man, you better than this." they entered the elevator. "I'm for real KT," said Leroy as he pressed the button. "My daughter and April are in trouble and all you can do is fucking drink."

"I know man I'm sorry for that but if you shut me out and…"

The door opens. "Let's go," Leroy said as the two stopped short at the door to Cox office. Leroy held the door knob but didn't turn it; he looked at KT. "Got gum?"

"No why?"

"Because you sure need it, here suck on this." Leroy gave him a piece of mint candy from out of his pocket.

"We need to get inside without being detected, if needed shoot to kill because he's arm and extremely dangerous." Belinda, Cox and some other officers were quietly going over their plans, on Cox desk where photos of the suspect's hide out and two indictments for James Shakespeare and Elizabeth Francis arrest. "No need to sit down," Cox said as Belinda and the other officers glanced over at KT and Leroy as they walked in. "Each team will have one detective and three patrol officers," Cox said. "We do have photos of the house," Cox continued as he hands Belinda a yellow folder and ask her to pass it around. "As you can see it's a large place to cover so once you're there call for any additional back up if you think you may need it." when Cox was done talking; he carefully check the names on the indictments, placed one in his back pocket and handed out the rest. "Warrants," Leroy blurted out. Belinda jumped. "Chill out." Leroy stood motionless. "We got to do this the right way Leroy you don't want to mess this up do you?" Leroy didn't answer, he just storm out the office and went out into the hallway. His eyes were red with anger, his body tense, he put his left hand under his arm and felt his piece. KT and Belinda went out after him but Leroy was already gone.

"I can't wait," said James. "As soon as Eve gets back we'll get started." April was butt ass naked, her arms and legs were tied together. Ball up in the middle of the floor, sweat dripping down from her ass cheeks. "Nice body," James said as he kneeled down to touch her, a cold chill immediately penetrate April skin causing her to jump. "Please!" she cried. "Please don't do this," she pulled at her restraints. James stood up over her. "You read Amy's letters? You saw the pictures," he folded his arms. "Now you understand why I'm doing this?" April tried to calm herself as she began talking. "It was mess up what he was doing to her."

"TO MY WIFE, WHAT HE WAS DOING TO MY WIFE!" he shouted as he marched around the room. "Every day I asked her to run away with me, so he would never find her." James stopped in front of April; he looked down and pointed his finger. "I should have stopped him the moment I found out who he was."

"You couldn't, he was too protected… he was a cop for crying out loud --- besides why didn't she just turn the pictures and letters over to the police instead of keeping them hidden away?"

"Well it's like what you said, he was too protected or have you forgotten how corrupt the Mecklenburg Police Department was back then?"

"Couldn't it been that she was too scared to say anything to the police?"

"Oh yeah right like you know --- you didn't know her."

"I didn't have too, I can tell from reading her letter's she was scared."

"Just shut up bitch!" he shouted with both hands over his ears. "You think you know it all --- don't you?" he charged around April, she turned her head in all directions to keep up with his movement. "Well it doesn't matter anymore she's dead and your baby daddy is responsible for it, and that's why the nigga is going to pay for it." April watched him disappear out the room, a few minutes later he came back holding a syringe. "What's that?" April asked in a terrifying tone. "Oh this here," he said sticking out the needle in front of his face. "This here is heroin, the same stuff that Detective Johnson has been pushing around the black neighborhood's for years, so now he's going to know how it feels to see someone he loves die from his own product." without warning James loomed over her, April squirmed trying to shake away but it was no use, all she could do was lay there helplessly. He lowered his body over hers, she smelled his breath kicking like dog shit, and she tried to pull at her restraints again. "Oh stop trying to fight it," he said with his eyes shining at her. When suddenly as if somebody had pushed the off button; he rose up, his legs were still spread out over her, he glanced back at the door and then looked down at April with a disappointed look on his face. He slowly lifted his left foot as he carefully stepped over her. "You'll going have to excuse me it sounds to me like we have company." with that he walked away, the door close leaving April still hog tie in the middle of the floor butt ass naked.

<u>Chapter 49</u>

Leroy stopped his car and leaned back in his seat as soon as he saw the woman turned into the driveway. He waited a few seconds and raised his head up just enough to see the lady get out the white Lincoln and go inside the house. He recognized the woman immediately; a couple blocks down the road DLT workers were getting prepared to lay down concrete at a nearby construction site, putting up signs and blocking off the area with their orange and yellow trucks. Leroy looked around at the house before pulling up behind the large vehicles. "Hey man you can't park your car there!" shouted a man wearing brown overalls and a yellow hard hat and steel toe boots. "Just be quiet and hop in," said Leroy as he reaches over to open the passenger side door. Inside the car Leroy showed him his badge. "I need you to help a nigga out, I'm trying to get inside that house down there," he pointed. "What size are those overalls you're wearing?" the man didn't answer. "What size Dammit?"

"36-40," the man replied. "That's what's up now get naked nigga."

"Come on man you tripping."

"Look nigga I'm not playing I need your shit."

"Man you crazy." Leroy pulled out his piece and stuck it in the man's face. "Nigga I'm giving you one more chance to come up out of them clothes or I'm going to blow your fucking brains out you understand me?" the man eyes got big. "Alright dog just chill with that okay." he began stripping down. After they were done switching out Leroy grabbed the hard hat and placed it on his head. "Now get out," Leroy said to the man who was now wearing his suit.

When Belinda and KT finally pulled up at the scene they noticed Leroy in his new outfit heading for the house. They started to get his attention but instead got out of the car and creep around the back of the house hoping to see where April and Kametica was being held. Leroy pulled the hat down over his eyes and walked up the front steps, he stood on the porch looking around over his shoulder with his pistol cuffed behind his back. He knocked on the door and inside a woman's voice said she was coming, when the lady answered the door she acted surprisingly startled when she saw Leroy standing there with an angry look on his face. "Where is he bitch?" she tried to slam the door shut but he pushes it back open. "Don't do that again, now were in the hell is he?"

"Sir I don't have no idea what you're talking about," she said as she tries to look around over Leroy shoulder hoping that there wasn't anybody else behind him. "Don't play games with me Eve or should I say Elizabeth Francis --- now I'm giving you one second to tell me where James is or I'm going to kill you right where you stand." Eve went silent for a moment and then spoke. "Alright I'll tell you," she said nervously. "He's in the basement cleaning, would you like me to go and get him for you?"

"Yeah right," without warning Leroy grabbed Eve's right arm and twisted it behind her and stuck his gun in her back. "We'll go holler at the nigga together like one big happy family." pushing the now frightened Eve in front of him they walked down into the basement, at the bottom he said. "Call him." Eve was trembling. "James!" no response. "Sometimes he can't hear too well."

"Call him again," he ordered. "James!" this time a man shouted back. "We got to get the hell out of here girl there's polices everywhere outside." Leroy stood behind Eve squeezing his grip. Coming around the corner of the basement James appeared. "What the fuck!" he was taken by surprise, Leroy pointed the pistol at Eve's head. "Don't move muthafucka or the white bitch is dead!" he shouted. James froze and held his hands up. "Where are they?"

"Who?"

"My daughter and April nigga don't act stupid."

"I don't know what the fuck you talking about." just then Belinda and other officers came running down the steps. "We found them Leroy they're fine, April is a little beaten up but she's alright." Leroy smiled --- you're lucky there's too many eyes boy because you'll be dead right now."

"Is that right?" James said smiling back as him and Eve were being hauled away in handcuffs by two police officers. Outside James was smirking and cussing at the crowd who had gathered around on the sidewalk to be nosy. "Put both of them in my car I'll be right back," Leroy said. The inside of the house was packed with detectives and patrol officers looking around. "Alright gentlemen the show is over clear out and let mobile crime do their thing," Leroy said as he entered, running over to April and Kametica he gave them both a big hug and kisses his daughter on the cheek. "It's all over now everything is okay." April was wrapped in a blanket, she held Kametica in her arms as the little girl cried uncontrollably. "This is your fault Leroy," April said hatefully. She shivered as she spoke. "He told me it was you who had Amy killed, and that you use your own brother to do it, and if it wasn't for his lady friend interrupting him when she did I would been…" Leroy put his hand on her shoulder. "I'm sorry April, there's a lot I haven't told you."

"Don't you touch me you damn bastard!" April said coldly. "I don't think I'll ever forgive you for this." Leroy looked at his daughter who was buried in her mother's arms. "Daddy is you coming home with us?"

 "I'm sure am honey as soon as I take the bad man to jail." his soft tone did a lot to calm the little girl who was no longer crying but still had tears coming down her face. April rocked her back and forth. "I have to take them down town, so I will tell Belinda to drive y'all home."

In the car Leroy looked through the review mirror at a grinning James and then at Eve who had her head down between her legs. Leroy cranks the car and peels out. He drove them to a nearby apartment complex, an area that was predominantly Hispanic and black. "Hey where in the hell are you taking us?" James asked. Leroy looked in the mirror at James who was now looking worried, he flips a switch and the sirens and the lights came on; cars and people scattered. He looked back at James through the cage. James face showed fear. "What's wrong James you look frightened?" Leroy said as the rolling lights reflected back into the car. "But don't worry this will all be over soon enough."

Chapter 50

Belinda had just got through talking to April and Kametica about their ordeal and was now taking them into her car when KT rushed over. "We just got a call from an off duty officer down on New Town Rd, said he saw Leroy riding through like a mad man on crack." KT had trouble catching his breath. "He also has the suspects."

"Are you for real?"

"Yup, and I don't think he's planning on taking them downtown either." Belinda got into her car and radio in to the Capt., she inform him on what was happening. "Do you think he's going to kill them?" April asked in the car. "I don't know April I just hope he comes to his senses."

"Well let's just go after him."

"No I can't --- my job is to take y'all home." when they made it to the house Kametica started back whining,

Belinda carried her inside and placed her on the couch, and she immediately fell to sleep. Belinda turned to April. "I'm alright Belinda honestly, just find Leroy because he's not thinking straight right now."

"Well I'm calling somebody over here now to keep an eye on y'all till…" her cell phone rang, it was Capt. Cox who said officers had spotted Leroy's car going down exit 221#. "Let me take care of this alone, he's just piss off right now I doubt he'd do anything stupid."

"Well okay I'm sending more back up, they'll stay clear until you give the call." Belinda rushed out the door, KT and other officers had already arrived so she requested them to stay guard. "Make sure that they don't leave the house," she said to KT then got into her car and drove off.

Holly Hills Park could be seen coming off 221#, a 1200 acre camp ground that was name after a civil rights leader in the 1960s, a one-way road went around the perimeter, parallel to it was a hiking trail which is usually pack with tourist and local folks. The territory has a large river bank, near it sat an old log cabin that looked like something off the Beverly Hill Billie's. It was a little dark and the cabin was empty, Leroy felt the floor squeak under his feet as he dragged a pleading James inside leaving an unconscious Eve in the car, throwing him across the floor Leroy immediately closed the front door and smiled. Still handcuffed James try to get to his feet but couldn't. "You won't get away with this Johnson," he said looking at Leroy. Leroy stood solidly, his legs width apart. "So!" he stared at James. "You shouldn't have put your hands on my family nigga."

"Well you shouldn't have killed my wife muthafucka!" James shouted back. With one large step Leroy was in front of James and then punched him in the mouth.

James fell back hitting his head up against the wall and he groaned. "Damn you and your wife!" James struggled to lean forward to catch his breath. "No, damn you nigga!" James said as he spits blood on Leroy pants leg. Leroy hit James again, this time the force made his front two teeth's fall out of his mouth. He was now bleeding badly, he looked up at Leroy. "Nigga you better go on ahead and kill me because if you don't I'm going to make sure that everybody knows what you really do for a living." Leroy's brow furrowed as he pulls out his pistol and cocks it. "Oh really?"

"Nigga I know about your dope connections in Mexico and the niggaz who sells it for you, I know Halley King was prostituting for you, who do you think sent them pictures to your Capt.?" James leaned back and laughs, the wall supporting his weight. "So go on ahead and shoot me muthafucka," James said burning his eyes into Leroy's. Leroy paced around as if he was not sure of himself. When suddenly a car pulled up, he knew it was Belinda. "Dammit!" he shouted. *"How in the hell did she know I was here?"* he said to himself. The high beams shone through the log cabin windows causing Leroy to block his eyes with his hand. "Belinda, stay the hell out of this!" He screamed out the door. Belinda slowly steps out the car. "Leroy please don't do this… he's not worth it --- trust me he's going to pay for what he did," she took a few steps closer. "Stop --- don't come any further or the nigga is a dead man." Leroy pointed his gun at James. "LEROY--- NOOO!!!" he fired and the bullet immediately hit James between the eyes, he felled to the floor dead as a door nail. Belinda rushed in and grabbed the gun out of Leroy's hand. "He shouldn't have touched my little girl Belinda, he shouldn't have touched her." Leroy looked dazed, his eyes lifeless, Belinda looked over at James who was curved up in a pool of blood. "Are you going to take me in?"

"No!" she said calmly. She looked at Leroy with glossy eyes. "Because to tell you the truth I would've done the same thing, that's why I'm giving you three hours to make a run for it, and after that you are on your own." Leroy smiled and gave her a huge. "Thank you Belinda."

"Now go... before I change my mine," she said as she waves him off for him to hurry on.

<u>Chapter 51</u>

The police at the Atlanta International Airport were scoping out the arriving passengers on the Charlotte Airway 185# from the Queen City, a man resembling Leroy Johnson's who was going by the name Vick

Logan with cash had bought a ticket, and according to an eyewitness decided not to board the flight, but what the witness didn't see however was that the same man returned minutes later dressed like a woman and got on the plane moments before the gateway door closed leaving behind his other cloths in the ladies room. During the flight Cox had called the Atlanta police station ten times to make sure that they were keeping an eye out for Leroy Johnson. When he was supposed to be in Atlanta Leroy was on the plane chilling, heading to Mexico.

"Have you heard anything from Leroy?" KT asked lighting up a cigarette. He and April were lying in the bed. "No, not recently but he did send a postcard to Kametica about a couple of weeks ago, saying that he was sorry and that he misses her."

"How is she taking it?"

"Not too good, her teacher has been telling me that the kids at school have been picking on her about her daddy, saying that he's a cold-blooded killer."

"Damn brats!"

"I know but they're probably right, he did murder James and had his wife killed."

"He's still a good guy."

"Come on now KT you don't really believe that, if you did you wouldn't be here fucking me behind his back." KT glanced at April, she caught his stare and she held it for an instant and averted her eyes; she continued. "All the years we have known each other I never thought he would stoop this low, leaving his daughter and me to provide for ourselves."

"You still have to give the man some credit he do send y'all money, it isn't like he have totally abandoned you."

"Maybe you're right I shouldn't be so resentful, besides its Tyrone who should be piss off at him because he's truly the only one paying the price in all this."

Epilogue

Overlooking the ocean in Cancun Mexico, now bald headed and only wearing a T-shirt and swimming shorts was reading a four-day old copy of the International News Journal. He took a lot of interest in a feature story about a police Captain being murder in Mecklenburg North Carolina. He leaned back in his chair, pulled down the brim on his sun visor and adjusted his shades; he sipped on his Corona and looked back down at the paper. The story quoted District of Mecklenburg Police Lieut. Belinda Bright who took a DNA sample from hair left on the victim's cloths, however when the results came back to a Troy Washington the authorities immediately arrested Troy known as A.K.A Smoke, and charge him with the murder of David Cox. *"We think we know who ordered the hit but we can't be sure until we find that person."* He took another sip and studied the sky, it looked like it was about to rain. A thick Mexican woman walk pass him and smiled. He started to get up and go holler at her but decided not to. He waited a moment before removing the story from the newspaper using a sharp end of his sunglasses. He folded it and placed it in his swim shorts. Leroy Johnson who was now going by the name Vick Logan closed his eyes. His hands place behind his head, the soft breeze carried the smell of fresh ocean water, and he slept in peace.

Ra' Un Seti

www.ingramcontent.com/pod-product-compliance
Lightning Source LLC
Chambersburg PA
CBHW060937120726
47910CB00002B/365